D0422394

Littlejim's Dreams

GLORIA HOUSTON

Littlejim's
Dreams

Illustrated by Thomas B. Allen

HARCOURT BRACE & COMPANY

San Diego   New York   London

Copyright © 1997 by Gloria Houston
Illustrations copyright © 1997 by Thomas B. Allen

All rights reserved. No part of this publication may
be reproduced or transmitted in any form or by any means,
electronic or mechanical, including photocopy, recording, or any
information storage and retrieval system, without
permission in writing from the publisher.

Requests for permission to make copies of any part
of the work should be mailed to: Permissions Department,
Harcourt Brace & Company, 6277 Sea Harbor Drive,
Orlando, Florida 32887-6777.

Library of Congress Cataloging-in-Publication Data
Houston, Gloria.
Littlejim's dreams / written by Gloria Houston;
illustrated by Thomas B. Allen.
p.   cm.
Summary: In 1920 in the mountains of western North Carolina,
fourteen-year-old Jim Houston sees his hopes of continuing his education
fade when his mother becomes seriously ill and his logger father must
deal with the underhanded dealings of outside businessmen.
ISBN 0-15-201509-4
[1. Fathers and sons—Fiction.
2. Mountain life—North Carolina—Fiction.   3. North Carolina—Fiction.]
I. Allen, Thomas B. (Thomas Burt), 1928—   ill.   II. Title.
PZ7.H8184Lj   1997
[Fic]—dc21   96-46338

Text set in Cloister Old Style
Designed by Linda Lockowitz

First edition
A C E F D B

Printed in the United States of America

To Jerry M. Houston,
simply the best

JUNIOR
HOUSTO

The author gratefully acknowledges
the help of the following in making this book:

Paula Wiseman, editor, mentor, listener, and friend

Sandy Yoo, messenger, listener

Addie Barrier, for information about wildflowers and grasses

Paul Cafferty, for information about horses and tack

Ruth Houston, for dialectical terms and cultural expertise

Frank Vance, for stories of Galen's exploits with Buffalo Bill

Milt Wiseman, for stories
of Harry's exploits with Barnum and Kennedy

Jerry Williamson, for his helpful book
*Hillbillyland: What the Movies Did to the Mountains
and What the Mountains Did to the Movies*

John Parris, for his "Roaming the Mountains" column
in *The Asheville Citizen-Times*

The Mountain Heritage Center,
Western Carolina University, Cullowhee, North Carolina

Chapter 1

"JIMMY. JIMMY," called Mama's voice from the kitchen. "Please come feed the pigs. The pail is full, and I am ready to peel the potatoes."

"I'll be along in a minute," Littlejim answered, shaking his head to throw the brown hair that hung down over his forehead back from his eyes. Sitting on the front steps of the pretty white house with green trim around the doors and windows, he contemplated for a moment longer the laces on the tall logging boots. They were exactly like those worn by Bigjim, his father and the best logger on Henson Creek. Each time he looked at the boots, he wondered if they were foretelling his future, if his future meant he too would be the best logger on the Creek. Although he had dreamed when he was younger of owning a fine team of Percherons like Scott and Swain and of being a fine logger like his papa, he was no longer sure that was the future he wished for himself.

Since he had won the *Kansas City Star*'s essay contest almost two years ago, just as the Great War ended, he had begun to dream other dreams. And ever since he had seen the wondrous airship last summer in Plumtree, his dreams had taken him far above the earth, beyond the steep hills and narrow valleys he called home in the plateau between the Blue Ridge and the Appalachian Mountains.

Sometimes his dreams had taken him to the big university library he had seen in one of his aunt Zony's magazines, a library filled with all sorts of books he longed to read. Sometimes his dreams had taken him high into the clouds, where he could see himself soaring and diving like the ravens he watched over the meadows on warm summer days, like the airship as he had watched it swoop down to land beside the river on Fourth of July last. Sometimes he even dared to dream that one day he might fly on an airship to other places he had read about, like New York City or Philadelphia. On rare occasions he even dared hope he might follow in Uncle Galen's footsteps to Montana, Arizona, or California.

It seemed that almost every day, news from the modern world added new details to the boy's dreams. These days Littlejim waited almost as eagerly as his father for the arrival of the *Kansas City Star*, which came up the mountain from Tennessee on a lumber train and then made its way in the mailman's sack to the Creek.

Uncle Galen was Bigjim's elder brother, and now that he had come back to the Creek to live, he sometimes shared his adventures, telling of the days when he rode with Buffalo Bill on the big buffalo hunts out west or how his company reached the Little Big Horn Valley one day after General Custer had met defeat at the hands of the great chief of the Oglala Sioux, Crazy Horse. Littlejim loved to listen to his uncle, and he dreamed of having just such adventures.

But Littlejim sighed. He supposed that he would have to settle for less exciting adventures than Uncle Galen's now that the Sioux had been forced to live on reservations. Just last week he had read in Aunt Zony's *New York Times* that Chief Crazy Horse was dead and that Buffalo Bill had died three years ago in 1917. The Great War—the war to end all wars, according to President Wilson—had been won and Germany had been defeated. It seemed that all the great adventures had happened before he was old enough to be a part of them, so Littlejim supposed he would have to go looking for others.

Turning over the book he had been reading and placing it open on the step beside him, Littlejim lifted his eyes from it to the sliver of white shining in the bright blue spring sky. Mr. Verne had written of men who traveled in a great airship to the moon. Perhaps one day he too would be one of the men who soared far above the earth. He stretched his long back against the post where Mama's English ivy wound itself around the white wood and tickled the side of his face. He chose to let his mind soar far above the white puffy clouds gathering between the twin peaks of the mountain the Cherokee had called the Spear Tops.

Just as he felt himself free to soar with the ravens, his thoughts brought him back to the steps of the Houston family home. First, he wanted so much to get out of the valley community of farms that bordered the Creek. He often dreamed of going away to an academy where he could get a better education than Mr. Osk could offer in the one-room school. He was by far the tallest, and the eldest, pupil in the school, attending every day his papa could spare him from the logging. There had to be a way, a way out of this valley, this home, this place he so loved, from which he had only traveled a few miles, the place where he had slept every night of his entire fourteen, almost fifteen, year life. He wrinkled his nose and sighed again. He had to find a way.

"Littlejim! Littlejim!" a voice intruded on his quiet thoughts. His younger sister Nell came running up the path that wound up the embankment and across the yard, shouting, "A letter! It's from the *Kansas City Star*!" In her excitement she dropped Bigjim's newspaper, its pages scattering across the frost-browned grass with the March wind sweeping down the valley. She frantically scurried to gather the sheets of newsprint as they swirled around her.

Trying not to betray his pounding heart, Littlejim sat up stiffly, thinking that recently every time he moved, his legs and arms seemed to have grown longer than the last time he moved them, leaving him with little control. He decided that he would be less apt to show his excitement if he sat still and let Nell chase the newspaper. As the eldest child and only son in the Houston family, Littlejim felt he could not afford to behave as childishly as his younger sister. He had almost proven to his father that he was, in Bigjim's words, "right much of a man," and he could not afford to jeopardize such status.

"A letter, you say?" he asked casually, the question beginning in his low manly voice, but ending in the little boy squeak he hated, as Nell handed the envelope to him. Examining the words printed in the top corner and savoring his own name written in a fine hand gave him a moment to take a deep breath. He needed to calm his shaking hands before taking out his pocketknife, a necessity in every Appalachian mountain boy's life, to open the blade to use as a letter opener.

"Read it, Littlejim. Read it, please," pleaded Nell, dancing a little dance of excitement on the brown grass. Dropping the envelope beside him, he unfolded the letter and glanced at the words. A smile started at his eyes and spread to his mouth, finally wrinkling up his nose as he indicated that Nell should sit beside him. Littlejim began to read.

"March 9, 1920
    "Dear Jimmy Houston,
"First, the entire staff joins me again in congratulating you on your fine winning essay in our Fourth of July competition two years ago. Your essay was one of the most popular items we have ever published. We have had numerous requests to repeat it, and we would like to do so in the near future, perhaps the week of the presidential election in November. Enclosed you will find the permission letter for your parent(s) to sign.
    "A second reason for this letter is to ask for your permission to enter your essay in a national competition with other winners from regional papers over the past two years. First prize for the national winner is a scholarship to an academy of your choice to complete your education and prepare you for entry into a good college. Permission papers for your entry in the national competition are also enclosed.
    "Again, congratulations on your fine work. Good luck.
    "Sincerely,
    "Alex Marshall, Publisher"

The boy sat for a moment, a wide grin stretching his face so the skin on his cheeks and chin felt as if it would break. Nell's grin was almost as wide. Throwing one arm around her brother's shoulders, she gave him a quick hug as she leaped up and ran around the porch to the kitchen door to share the good news with Mama.

Maybe, just maybe, Littlejim thought, his dreams might come true. As a thousand pictures of all the possibilities of his future scurried across his mind, the grin he still wore grew wider. Then that grin spread down through his whole body. When it reached his feet, he leaped off the steps, threw his arms into the air, and dancing around, first on one foot and then on the other, shouted to the bright winter sky above, "I'll be a scholar! I'll be an aviator! I'll travel all the way to the moon! I'm going to be somebody! I'm going to the academy, maybe even on to the university!"

"You fool boy! What is this dern racket all about?" Suddenly Littlejim's feet and heart stopped with a thud, as a tall, gaunt man in sawdust-covered overalls and slouch hat pulled low over his eyes opened the gate to the wood yard. A scowl darkened the man's face and drew his lips into a thin line. As he spoke, he seemed to growl.

Not waiting for an answer, his father continued to talk as Littlejim quickly slipped the letter into the back pocket of his pants. "Seems a no-account boy can't find enough to do around the place. Has plenty of time to sit around reading and enough energy to break a man's ears with that infernal racket." He leaned down beside Littlejim to pick up his newspaper where Nell had left it on the top step. "See if you can't fetch the pail and go slop the hogs. It's feeding time, and I heard your ma tell you that she needed you to empty the slop bucket as I drove the horses into the barn. Now stop this wool-gathering and move!"

Stumbling as he moved toward the kitchen door, Littlejim nearly forgot the letter stuffed in his pocket. The happiness the letter had brought ended like a thunderclap as his father's words stung his ears, as tears of disappointment stung his eyes.

Chapter 2

AS LITTLEJIM OPENED the kitchen door, he saw Mama stirring batter and smiling broadly as she scraped the sides of the bowl.

Nell was cleaning applesauce from May's chin each time the younger girl missed her mouth. Littlejim smiled at the scene. He often had to remind himself that May, now three, going on four, years old, did not like to be called Baby May. She saw herself as a real person, not the baby of the family. She reminded her brother of one of the honeybees in Papa's hive, scurrying around the house and yard, her voice a constant drone of happy chatter or the merry tunes she made up as she busied herself exploring her world.

Standing in the open doorway, the boy watched the chill wind blowing Mama's apron and thought that the kitchen at his house around supper time was surely the best place in the world to be.

"Ach, my fine essay writer," said Mama, interrupting

his thoughts. "Were you raised in a barn? Or might you close the door so the heat will stay inside?" He smiled sheepishly.

"Littlejim was raised in the barn with Scott and Swain," sang May, and then burst into a fit of laughter at her own joke.

"Na, na, na, na, na, na," sang Nell. "But he writes prize-winning essays anyhow."

Closing the door, Littlejim walked around the table to pull one of Nell's braids and tweak May's nose as he watched a lump of soft white dough slide from Mama's mixing trough to a flour-covered cloth. Mama rolled the dough into a flat circle, dipped a drinking glass into the cloth sack of flour standing nearby, and quickly turned the glass upside down to cut enough biscuits to fill the large black pan waiting on the stove.

Passing between Mama and the stove so she could not see what he was doing, Littlejim quickly snatched one of the biscuits from the pan and began to nibble.

"Yah, Jimmy," said Mama, slapping at his hands with her flour-covered ones. "You are a boy with hollow legs! It is not enough food I can cook to fill them. You eat the biscuits before I can get them into the oven!"

"Why are we having biscuits for supper? Papa likes corn bread," said Littlejim.

"A hog was butchered for Tarp this morning, so he sent us fresh tenderloin for supper. Such a treat calls for biscuits," said Mama. "And Zony sent us some flour from their fine crop of wheat, new from the mill this morning. Too it is deserving that I am cooking a feast to celebrate the success of my fine son, the essay writer, don't you think?"

Littlejim grinned and stopped chewing long enough to give his mother a hug. He was startled to realize that he was a head taller than she was. He did not remember having been this tall when he had hugged her only a few weeks ago.

"A fine pot of wild greens, found by Fayette's boys by the creek, simmer on the stove," Mama continued. "Potatoes roast in the tenderloin's drippings. What a fine feast we will have in celebration this evening! Now, my son, sit down and read your letter to me. Nellie says it has good news."

"Papa wants me to slop the hogs," he said, his mouth watering as he contemplated the taste of fresh greens. Any green vegetable was welcome after a long winter's diet of root vegetables and dried beans, but the season's first greens were among the best things about spring, or so Littlejim thought.

"The hogs can wait," said Mama, sitting demurely on the end of the bench beside the table and tilting her head slightly to one side as she always did when she listened intently. "This letter we will hear first."

Littlejim slung one booted foot across the bench and sat astride it as he reached back to take the sheet of paper from his pocket and unfold it. Then he began to read.

When he had finished, Mama said, "Oh, my fine

son. It is a scholar you shall be—a scholar like your Opa, my father. Or perhaps you will one day teach at a university like your onkle Hans back in the old country. It is very proud of you this day I am."

"I don't know," said Littlejim, squirming, suddenly growing shy as Mama reached out to push his hair back from his eyes as she had done when he was a small child.

Taking his chin in her hand, Mama looked directly into his eyes and, speaking softly, said, "My fine son, dream your fine dreams. Give up your dreams never. Without dreams, life has no direction. The starting point for everything, our dreams are. If you are to go somewhere, first you must dream. Promise me, my son."

"I promise, Mama," whispered Littlejim, wishing he could always feel her small warm hand on his face.

Then standing suddenly and opening the oven door to check on the biscuits, Mama added, "But for the moment, it is the chores you must tend to. The biscuits are browning."

Folding the letter, Littlejim placed it carefully under the sugar bowl in the middle of the table as Mama opened the door of the dry sink and handed him the pail of table scraps, reminding him as always, "Put on your wrap. It is your death of cold you'll catch since the sun has gone down."

Chapter 3

LATER THE FAMILY sat around the table, heads bowed, while Bigjim said a prayer of thanks for the food, followed by a booming "Amen."

May imitated him in her tiny voice. "A-hem!" she said, giggling and pounding her spoon on the table. Nell and Littlejim laughed, to May's great delight.

Bigjim ignored the merriment and passed the bowls of food. Filling his plate, he began to eat with his head lowered, so his son could not see his expression, although the boy watched carefully, trying to find the right moment to share his good news. He wanted to make sure Bigjim received the letter as *good* news.

Mama brought the black baking pan from the oven and passed the hot, fragrant biscuits. Handing an extra one to Nell, she said, "Open it and let it cool so May will not get burned."

Then placing the pan on the stove, she took a biscuit for herself and sat down. Passing the apple butter, she said, smiling, "James, some news we have to share, some very happy news."

Bigjim seemed to growl. "Best news I could hear is that lumber prices are rising," he said, as if he had not heard his wife. Then he lifted his head to glower at the family and added, "Instead, word around the sawmill is that the Mortimer Lumber Company is moving its big band mills into the county. People like Bob and me, we'll be out of business. We'll go broke." He shook his head sadly. "The times, they are changing so fast a man can't keep up."

Littlejim felt his hunger leave him, replaced by a hollow feeling that had nothing to do with food. Everyone at the table—except May, who was happily humming her little tune as she chewed her biscuit—sat in silence.

"James, good news and bad, it is all easier to take on a full stomach," said Mama firmly. "My good biscuits will prepare us for whatever lies ahead, both good and bad. Now eat." And she picked up her fork to follow her own command. Littlejim and Nell followed her example.

Feeling his appetite returning, Littlejim soon cleaned his plate and stood to pass more biscuits to his family. Finally he found the courage to ask his father exactly what the coming of the big sawmills meant to the Houston family.

"It means a man won't have a way to earn a dollar of hard cash," Bigjim said. "These woods will be grubbed. There won't be a live stick standing."

Littlejim prepared several biscuits filled with apple butter, which he planned for dessert, and poured himself some milk from the pitcher.

"You got holler legs, boy," said Bigjim. "You won't be able to eat like that when the big companies get through. What you eat, you'll have to grow, just like we did when I was boy."

Littlejim was confused. He had fed the hogs to provide the tenderloin when Tarp had gone to market. He had helped Uncle Pierce cradle the wheat from which the flour was made. He could remember having had a part in producing everything they had for supper except the greens, which grew wild near the creek. He did not understand how a big company moving into the county would change their lives very much, but his father's dour countenance and ominous words overwhelmed the boy, making him forget the great joy of his own good news.

Remembering the letter hidden under the sugar bowl, Littlejim glanced at Mama to see her reaction, but she continued eating, looking steadily at her husband as Bigjim reached one long arm across the space to the stove to help himself to another biscuit and then poured himself a second cup of coffee.

Finally Mama sat tall, rising to her full height in the chair, and said in a commanding voice, "James, our son has brought so good news this day, news which will off-set the bad news about the timber."

Bigjim looked first at his son, then at his wife, "What's that fool boy done now?" he asked.

Littlejim felt his heart sink to his feet. He had thought his father might be pleased at the news, but he should have known better.

"Our son is a fine writer and scholar," said Mama, with determination underlining every word. "He has been asked to place his fine essay, the prize-winning one, in a greater competition with pupils from all over the country. At stake is a scholarship to an academy. Is that not fine news, James?"

Littlejim watched Mama looking intently at her husband, almost willing her husband to agree with her.

"He wants to go away to an academy and study?" asked Bigjim, his eyes making narrow slits above his mustache. "Logging's not good enough for him?"

Mama bristled. "Logging is a fine occupation," she said. "Do you not provide us a fine living cutting timber, James? But not every man is a logger in his heart. Some men are scholars. I think that our son, in his heart, is a scholar. And is that not a fine thing to be, too?"

"Schooling's fine," said Bigjim. "I never got much, and I regret that. But schooling's best if a man's work is not there to do. And it looks like a man's work won't be long in these hills. Mayhap he needs to find another way to make a living."

Littlejim was not sure if that meant his papa approved of his entering the competition but, after a glance at Mama, he decided that he had received as much approval from Papa as he would get this day. Picking up one of his apple-butter—stuffed biscuits, he savored the taste of the food on his tongue and then the feel of the cold milk as he swallowed. The room was silent except for the sounds of eating and of May's soft little song of happiness.

Littlejim dared to let himself imagine again sitting in a big university library surrounded by books, then he allowed his mind to soar to imagine what the earth must look like from the great airship he would pilot one day. In his mind he could see his family waving from the yard of the house on the Creek as he passed over, and he could see his papa pointing upward to show his friends that it was *his* son flying so high, *his* son who piloted that plane high in the air for all to see. Littlejim smiled happily as he imagined what his papa would say at the gathering on some future Sunday morning. "Why, that's my boy," his father would say. "My boy went to the university, and then he learned to fly—"

The boy's dream was interrupted. There was a hurried knock on the kitchen door, as if someone could hardly wait to get inside.

Chapter 4

LITTLEJIM, SEATED near the door, stood up to open it as the knock sounded again. Opening the door, he realized that he was taller than Uncle Bob, who stood in front of him, blowing on his fingers, trying to warm them. He wore neither coat nor hat, having left both behind in his eagerness to talk with his brother.

Bigjim turned slightly. "Come in, brother," he said. "Gertrude has made some fine biscuits this supper time."

Mama scurried to set a place for Uncle Bob beside her husband.

"Don't mind if I do," said Uncle Bob, taking the cup of coffee offered by Mama. "This'll warm a body on a cold night. No time to eat all day. A biscuit would surely taste right good, I reckon."

Accepting the plate Mama offered and beginning to eat with great enthusiasm, Uncle Bob said between bites, "I guess you heard the news, Jim?"

"Heard it, but ain't digested it all yet," said his older brother. "Not good news for any of us in these hills, I reckon."

"But, Jim, it could be good news for all of us," argued Bob. "We just contract ourselves, our horses, and our machines out to Mortimer while they are cutting in this county. Then when they leave, we go back to our old way of doing things. In the meantime, we have made us some cash money to buy new, more, and better machinery."

Angrily Bigjim shoved back his chair and stood up, leaned over, and grasped the edge of the table. "Bob, you fool! You are all caught up in this frenzy for change!"

Littlejim watched as his father began to pace, growing more agitated with every word.

"Have you listened to Galen talk about his travels out west?" Littlejim heard his father ask. "Have you listened to your new gaffer, Ian McIntosh, talk about the hills back in Scotland? Have you not heard what these men are saying to us?"

May jumped as her father pounded on the table to accent his words, making the dishes and cutlery rattle. Startled, she stared in surprise at her father.

Bigjim pounded the table again in frustration. "Brother, do you not hear me?" He shouted.

"I hear you. I hear you," said Uncle Bob placatingly. "Good thing about timber. Leave a few seedlings, and it always grows back. Meanwhile, we have pocket money to make improvements so we can make more when the big companies leave."

Bigjim threw up his hands, his fingertips touching the ceiling, the galluses of his overalls stretching on his tall frame as he slapped the ceiling in his exasperation.

Littlejim had never in his life seen his father more upset. He looked across the table at Nell, whose face was still and fearful. Mama stood beside the stove, waiting—for what Littlejim was not sure.

Finally his father walked out of the kitchen into the hall, then abruptly turned back into the room to face his brother, who had cleaned his plate and was draining the last drops from his coffee cup.

"Now, brother, listen to me and listen good." Bigjim's voice shifted to an intense whisper as he sat down and leaned toward Uncle Bob, pointing his finger at his brother in a most unmannerly way. "Galen told us—you were there, you heard him—that the big lumber companies out in the West cut everything big enough to make a broom handle and left the land naked to wash away the soil so's nothing decent can grow again."

Littlejim was horrified. He could see a picture in his mind of Spear Tops Mountain without the forests covering its sides, looking like Eli Buchanan's bottomland after the fire got out in the broomsage there last fall, the rich soil washing away in the rain to leave hard clay, red and barren.

"We have virgin forests here, Bob," continued Bigjim. "We still have boundaries of timber with a few trees twelve, fifteen feet across the stump in this part of the country. Trees that size have been cut almost every place else. We have trees as big as any in the United States except them big redwoods I read about out in Californy. When the lumber companies from *off* get through, we'll have no more than a patch of weeds. You know how long it takes to grow a tree that size. Our grandchildren will not live long enough to see trees that size again."

"Yes," Uncle Bob answered. "And you know how much some of your big trees in the Charl Ollis Cove will bring on the stump, or even better, as dressed lumber." Moving his fingers in the air, he began to calculate numbers in his head, ignoring his brother's message.

"And I don't intend to cut those trees in the cove unless it's a *have-to* case. That's one of the last stands of virgin timber left anywhere. We have destroyed most of the virgin growth here. We don't cut and burn anymore like our grandsires done, but the damage they did won't be undone in our lifetime," said Bigjim. "Or our children's. We keep on, and this place will look just like the deserts Galen talks about out west where nothing grows but cactus, or this place will be like the high hills in Scotland, fit only for briars."

Littlejim was thinking of Ian McIntosh's description

of the Scottish highlands at noonday dinner Saturday last at Uncle Bob's sawmill.

"Ian says the Scottish hills used to be forested like these," Littlejim said suddenly, speaking more loudly than he had intended, hoping to help his father make Uncle Bob listen to reason. "He says that over the past two hundred years, the forests there have been cut clean so that no trees were left to reseed. He says that now the hills are barren except for the bracken, which even the sheep won't eat."

"Hold your tongue, boy," barked Bigjim. "This is a man's argument. Ain't no call for a boy to interfere."

"Sheepherding might be a good business around here once the big timber is cut," mused Uncle Bob, not hearing either of them. "Some of our grandsires raised sheep. Mutton brings a good price on the Piedmont market. Makes a fine stew, too."

"One of these days these hills will be as barren as the hills of Scotland in the pictures Ian brought with him to the Creek," said Bigjim. "Are you hearing me?"

Littlejim was startled to hear his contribution to the argument repeated by his father, when he had only moments before been told to hold his tongue. But when his inquiring look caused Mama to shake her head and place one index finger over her lips as warning, he decided not to remind his father that he was repeating his son's words.

"Then we'll all be out of a living. Nothing will grow fit for anything short of a goat to eat. Then you'll be saying, 'Why didn't I see it coming?' Well, brother, don't say I didn't warn you!" Bigjim took his hat off the peg beside the door and, throwing his heavy sweater across one arm, opened the door, letting the cold wind blow into the warm kitchen.

At last he turned to face his family, saying, "Brother, you are not using the good sense God gave a goose," said Bigjim. "This cutting frenzy has turned your head. Don't say I didn't warn you!" And he slammed the door behind him.

"Jim will see the light in time. When the rest of us are making a good living without working so hard, he'll come around. 'Trude, any more of your good biscuits left?" asked Uncle Bob. "Yes, sir, Littlejim, big changes are coming."

As his father had said, times were changing very fast, so fast Littlejim could hardly keep up. He had always wished for change. He loved the things from *off*, things from the world so far from his valley. He hoped that aeroplanes, auty-mobiles, and all the wonders from the newspapers he read would one day be a part of his life.

But now he was not so sure if Uncle Bob was right. Or if his father might be thinking more clearly than his uncle. This time Littlejim was very confused about who was right.

Chapter 5

NEWS WAS BUZZING up and down the Creek Road that the Mortimer Lumber Company had moved into the north end of the county, had set up its sawmills there, and was expanding the rail line from Tennessee deep into the forests. Agents had set up hiring tables at Vance's Store and were beginning to hire men around Plumtree for their crews. High wages of as much as one dollar per day provided an incentive for local men to leave their small farms to move to the timber camps, a day's journey by horseback or wagon.

Word was that Mr. Burleson had refused to allow the agents to recruit at his store because he held the same opinion as Bigjim, that cutting the heavy virgin forests of the Greater Appalachians would not well serve the small mountain farmers and their self-sufficient way of life.

One of Mr. Burleson's sons, away to study history at college, often wrote long letters to his proud father, which were shared with all who would listen. Mr. Burleson explained that the Appalachian Mountains had been the first American frontier, crossed by pioneers before the colonies became a nation. Those who stayed to settle in the 1700s instead of following their brothers and sisters to the West brought their European traditions with them. They stayed to fell great trees, to build cabins, to clear fields for crops, and to create a self-sufficient way of life common to all frontier populations as settlers moved west. For the next two hundred years the southern mountaineers, like those who lived in the North Toe River Valley, like the residents of the Henson Creek community, had kept their self-sufficient farm life alive, even as it had been disappearing in the rest of the United States. Mr. Burleson took his son's words seriously and took a stand against the big lumber companies.

Preacher Hall agreed. He often said that the southern mountaineer "lived at home and boarded at the same place." Growing one's own food, making one's own clothing, creating one's tools, needing to buy only coffee or some other treat not native to the area: being self-sufficient was a way of life that as an outsider—a person whose family had lived in the valley for only *one* generation—the preacher, or so he said, certainly admired.

Whenever Bigjim drove the team and wagon into the village to pick up supplies, he, Mr. Burleson, and

Preacher Hall held long discussions about the changes that had been coming to the mountains and its people since the Great War. They always ended by agreeing that things did not need to change, that things were fine just the way they were.

They also agreed that mining was an acceptable occupation. After all, mining for mica and other minerals had been a part of the valley since it was Cherokee land. The Tar Heel Mica Company in Plumtree, they agreed, was not part of the big changes that worried them, because the mica industry provided work for those not really suited to farming or who needed more hard cash than farming could provide.

Littlejim was not sure what he thought about the changing life in the valley. He and Andy McGuire had been reading Jules Verne's stories about the world of the future, but none of them considered what might happen if all the great forests were cut. Nor, according to Bigjim, did his books deal with the processing of minerals found in the valley where Littlejim's family had lived for the past five generations, since the land there had belonged to England. So, although the boys found no answers in Mr. Verne's books, his books contained some of the most exciting ideas they had found and which they delighted in discussing at every opportunity.

Many of their new ideas came from Mr. Verne's books, but almost as many were gleaned from Bigjim's *Star* and Aunt Zony's *Times*, which the two friends read eagerly as soon as the grown-ups were finished. Each newspaper was filled with articles about new inventions and improvements on old ones, such as the engines that would run a speedy fifty miles an hour or more, and records set and broken by racehorses and athletes. One editorial in the *Times* used the speed of new accomplishments to demonstrate that indeed the twentieth century was off to a running start and would be the century to change the world—for the better, of course. Like Mr. Verne's books, the articles failed to address the issues of demolishing great forests and mining minerals from the earth or what their loss might mean to the people of the future.

Hardly realizing that the issues about which they read were of a world far removed from their own, Andy and Littlejim spent each evening after chores, when they could steal time to meet on the porch or in one family's kitchen, in heated discussions. They wondered what the future of the new century might hold for them and for the world of which they dreamed of being a part. Those discussions were becoming increasingly rare, however, because Andy was often absent from school and could rarely leave his house in the evening. Since his father was killed in the sawmill accident almost three years ago, his mother had kept the farm going with help from Andy and a few good neighbors. In the daytime his mother cleaned houses for ladies in the village, so Andy often stayed home to do the farm chores and care for the younger children. Evenings found him doing heavy farm chores or helping his mother, who came home too tired to care for the cows, pigs, and chickens. Occasionally, however, the two boys still found time to share books, and Andy found some time to read.

One chilly spring morning Mr. Osk had asked the two oldest boys in the school to mend the fence between the school yard and Mr. Pittman's pasture. As they had all through the winter, the friends argued as they replaced the boards and drove nails carefully into the fence posts, about whether Mr. Verne's idea of building a ship that could carry people underwater was possible or not. Finally they agreed that such an underwater ship might be possible.

However, they disagreed with great energy about their favorite author's story about riding a ship through the sky to the moon. Littlejim believed that someday, certainly not in his lifetime, he was sure, but someday, humans might go to the moon and beyond. After all, he had seen an aeroplane with his very own eyes, and he had tried to fly the one he built last summer. He believed that one day humans might fly even farther than he could imagine. Andy was just as sure that such a journey was impossible, no matter how far into the future their imaginations might help them to see.

"I think that someday a man will walk on the moon," argued Littlejim, cutting a board to fit the hole in the fence.

"No," replied Andy. "That aeroplane we saw last summer is as far as a man will ever go up into the air."

"I don't think so," said Littlejim, placing the board carefully against the rail. "Someday humans will go farther still, to places we don't even know exist. Oh, how I would like to be one of them!"

"Not me," said Andy, pounding a nail into the top rail. "I want to go to the coalfields of West Virginia. I want to go underground. I've heard tell that a man can make double there what he makes cutting timber here. Wages are real good. If I can just get a job in the coal mines, then maybe my ma won't have to clean for other people and take care of all of us, too."

"Mining has no hold on me," said Littlejim. "It's dangerous. Papa's cousin Hoyle worked in the mines. He tried to get Papa to let me quit school and join him. I was glad Papa was stubborn that time, because Hoyle lost his legs in a cave-in. I don't want to quit school, either."

"Neither do I," said Andy. "But no doubt I'll have to sooner or later. Ma is sacrificing a lot so I can come the few days I manage to make now. I will miss reading and talking about books with you when I leave, Littlejim. Seems like that's the best thing about school."

Littlejim placed the hammer and nails back into the wooden tray Mr. Osk had loaned them to mend the fence. Walking back to the schoolhouse door, Littlejim

realized that they were both taller than any other pupils in the school. And he was a head taller than Mr. Osk.

Andy interrupted his thoughts. "Littlejim, you be sure to let me know how you come out in the competition. I am a mite jealous of you getting to go on, but you are the best scholar in the school. I guess my pa's getting killed put to rest any hopes I had of more learning than I can get here."

"Maybe you can go back to school later, and there are lots of ideas you can find in books, like the ideas of Mr. Verne," said Littlejim. "And if I should win, I don't know how Papa will feel about my going away. I'm not sure he was listening when Mama told him about the competition."

"He will let you go," said Andy. "I'm sure he is proud of you."

"Thank you, Andy," said Littlejim, shaking his friend's hand and placing one foot on the steps to enter the school as the clatter of horse's hooves sounded on the Creek Road. The boys turned just in time to see Tarp and his horse clear the top of the rail fence as he shouted, "Jimmy. Jimmy. Come quick. Gertrude's took sick. Bad sick. And we can't find Jim. He's in the woods."

Chapter 6

A S TARP REINED IN the horse, he reached down to lift Littlejim to sit behind him. Placing his foot into the stirrup Tarp had vacated for him, the boy barely made it to a sitting position on the horse's rump as Tarp urged the horse over the fence again.

"What's wrong with Mama?" Littlejim asked, the wind and his fear almost choking his words.

"Don't know," shouted Tarp over the sound of the horse's hooves. "I found her on the ground near the springhouse, face white and body bent double with pain. Bob sent one of his men for Doc Sloop and another to find Jim."

Digging his fingernails into the palms of his hands, wrapped tightly around his cousin's waist, Littlejim prayed that his Mama would be all right, whispering his plea as the horse and riders rounded the curve at Uncle Bob's sawmill. He would give anything to have his mama waiting, smiling and healthy, when they arrived home.

Then he saw as they passed that the men from the sawmill had stopped their work and gathered near the road, their faces grave. His heart sank.

Springing from the saddle as they stopped in the barnyard, Littlejim bounded over the wood-lot fence, his long legs carrying him up the front steps in two giant leaps. He opened the door and looked into the front room, where his parents' bed sat in the corner.

Mama's face, drawn and gray against the white sheets, looked very small as he stood in the doorway. Her eyes were closed, and he could not see if she was breathing. At her side stood a tall man with a graying beard. Sitting in the rocking chair near the bed was a tiny lady with a kind face, holding Mama's hand. Bigjim sat in a chair nearby, his shoulders stooped, his head in his hands.

"How is she?" asked Littlejim.

"She is feeling some better," said the lady. As she smiled, Littlejim recognized her. She was Emma's mother, the doctor who had covered his hands with ointment when they were frozen three winters ago. All that seemed so long ago, when he was a little boy. He thought the man must be Dr. Mr. Sloop, her husband.

He moved to stand at the foot of the bed. "What's wrong with her?" he asked.

"We can't be sure," the man said. "Doctor and I were discussing the best course of treatment. For now, we have given her something to make her sleep. It will help the pain."

"Could I speak to her?" Littlejim asked, his heart pounding.

"Of course," the lady doctor said. "But she may not hear you. She needs to sleep now. You will be able to talk to her in the morning."

Dr. Mrs. Sloop walked around the bed to lay her hand on Littlejim's arm. "We'll take as good care of her as we know how. She is our friend, too, you know. Why don't you go chop some wood for the kitchen so we can start a pot of soup? She will need to eat when she wakes up."

Stumbling to the front door, Littlejim turned to look back at his parents. He had never seen his father look defeated before this moment. The man had always been one to order others around, a man no one could please, a person who was always in charge and could do everything. But Littlejim knew that there were some things even his strong father could not change.

As he picked up the ax and placed a stick of wood on the chopping block, he looked up at the sky. It had not changed since he and Andy had talked in the school yard only a short while ago. This morning when he had left for school, Mama had been smiling as she waved at him. Now she was very sick, and even his big strong papa seemed frightened by her illness. Littlejim felt as if centuries had passed, and the whole world he had always known had changed.

Chapter 7

AS THE LAST DAYS OF MARCH passed into early April, Mama slowly grew stronger. The tonic Dr. Mr. Sloop had given her seemed to help her sickness. Although Dr. Mrs. Sloop came by every few days, Mama's disease had never been given a name, so Littlejim did not know what was wrong, but he knew she was still very sick because her face was the sort of gray of cold winter skies and his father's face never lost its expression of worry and sadness.

One of Mama's younger sisters, Geneva, from over the mountain in the Cane Creek community, a short lady with coal black hair and twinkling blue eyes who looked very much like Mama, came to help out with the family. Because she had been born in America, her speech had less of a lilt than Mama's, and she pronounced her words so they sounded more like those spoken by the Creek residents who, like Littlejim and Nell, had been born there.

Aunt Geneva had been a teacher, and she said she had less of an accent than her older sister, born in the old country, but she looked so much like Mama that Littlejim found himself expecting his merry little aunt to begin her sentences with "Yah, but..."

Sometimes Nell whispered that the food did not taste like Mama's when Aunt Geneva cooked it, but Littlejim refused to acknowledge her words, fearing to hurt his aunt's feelings. Perhaps fearing, too, that his aunt would go home and leave the cooking to them. Anything she made was sure to taste better than the biscuits he and Nell had made the day after Mama became ill. The biscuits were, in Bigjim's words, hard enough to kill a bull across the road. May gnawed away at hers, proud of what her new teeth could do. Bigjim soaked his in his saucer of coffee, grumbling throughout the meal, but managing to eat it. After that experience, Littlejim was only too happy to have Aunt Geneva cook for them.

Sometimes the boy stayed out of school to help his aunt with the care of his mother. When it was Nell's turn to stay home, Littlejim volunteered to work in her place so his sister could attend school regularly. He reasoned that she had been in school fewer years than he had, and he soon realized that he was the only one in the house who was strong enough to lift his mother into a chair for her bath and place her gently back on the feather mattress when the bed had been made. He was surprised the first time he lifted her. She weighed so little that he felt as if he were lifting May. How proud he was that his arms were strong enough to be trusted to lift his mama and to gently make sure she was comfortable in her chair. At those times, he felt a great lump in his throat, which seemed about to overwhelm him, but he could not determine if what he felt was love for Mama or fear of losing her.

He had no one with whom he could talk about his overwhelming feelings. He enjoyed conversations with his aunt, but Mama was the only one who seemed to understand feelings as intense as those he experienced when he was worried about Mama. And he could not tell her now.

Little by little, Littlejim realized he had less time for his dreaming or, so he thought, fewer possibilities for ever pursuing those dreams. The work of his family had to come first. If Mama's illness continued to be as serious as he thought it might be, he might have to postpone going away to school, even if he were lucky enough to win the scholarship. When he had time to think about postponing all the things he hoped would be a part of his future, he felt as if a heavy weight descended on his shoulders and on his spirits. But there was no one who could brighten his mood, as Mama had always brightened each day in some way for every member of his family.

Both Nell and Littlejim were surprised that Aunt

Geneva was such a cheerful, funny lady. She loved to tease them, and she always made jokes with them. She could make the children laugh, even when they were saddened by Mama's illness. Sometimes they heard a chuckle from Mama as her sister helped her bathe or fed her soup.

After Aunt Geneva reminded the children that she had learned in church that "a merry heart is good medicine," they saved funny incidents that happened at school or the errors they made helping with the house-work to share with Mama during their afternoon visits after school. Mama seemed stronger then, and some-times they made her smile.

One story that made her laugh softly when Littlejim told it was about the day he found a can of cherries that had spoiled. Thinking the cherries would be a treat for the chickens, he had poured them into the feed trough near the chicken coop, had washed the jar out in the springhouse, and returned to the kitchen with an arm load of stove wood. A short time later, Nell returned from gathering the eggs shouting that something was wrong with the chickens. They could not walk straight, and some of them fell down each time they tried to walk.

Mama always laughed at his story, and Aunt Geneva would comment wryly that "This family doesn't make pickled eggs. It pickles the chickens and lets them lay the eggs."

Nell did not understand the joke until Littlejim

explained that the fermented cherries had made the chickens quite drunk, so they were "pickled." Then Nell and May almost fell off their chairs laughing. Mama joined in the merriment with a happy smile, which made Littlejim's heart leap.

Bigjim hardly spoke to anyone. After supper each night he would take the lamp into Mama's room, stir up the fire in the fireplace, sit in the rocking chair close to her bed, and read, slowly and haltingly, with Mama.

Littlejim wanted to ask Papa if Mama's illness would keep him from going away to school next year, if he should win the scholarship. Sometimes, as he took more and more responsibility for the work around the farm, he felt as if all his dreams were just impossibilities. Each time he got up his nerve to talk to Bigjim about the letter without Mama's help, he decided that such questions would only burden his father until Mama's health was in a better state. How she was doing, however, seemed to be a question no one could answer, for each time Littlejim asked for information about Mama's illness, his papa turned away and said, "The Lord knows, son. The Lord knows."

And each time he heard those words, Littlejim's stomach turned into an empty, lonely, hollow place, even after supper when it was filled with Aunt Geneva's good food.

Chapter 8

THE WINTER PASSED and at last spring was coming. Littlejim knew that because Mama's daffodils, which the folks on the Creek called "Easter flowers," were peeping yellow heads through the last remnants of snow around the gray stones jutting out of the ground in the meadow above the road. Warmed by the afternoon sun, the flowers in the front yard showed bright green leaves accented here and there by sunny yellow trumpets heralding the coming of spring.

On his way home from school Littlejim had stopped to pick a bouquet of daffodils for Mama's room when he heard his mother's voice. He smiled with joy that she was strong enough to sit on the front porch and visit with someone. As he walked up the path, he recognized his favorite aunt's voice.

"Yes, Zony," Mama said. "I grow stronger each day. Soon I will be walking to your house again. Geneva says we can take the young man as a boarder for the summer."

Littlejim was delighted to see his aunt, Bigjim's only sister, sitting on the front porch. She had been his first teacher, and she was his good friend. She loaned him books from her collection, and when he returned them to her house, she took the time to talk with him about what he had read. During the past winter he had missed her terribly, for she had been away, tutoring the children of a wealthy family, so it was said.

"He is a law student," continued Aunt Zony's voice. "He is the son of one of my classmates at Mercer, when I went down to Macon as a young girl. A finer person I never knew than his mother, but I wanted to talk something over with you before you agree to take him as a guest."

"He sounds like a fine young man," said Mama.

"He is not of our religion, but that will affect your family very little," said Aunt Zony.

Mama gathered more energy than Littlejim had seen from her in weeks as she answered Aunt Zony abruptly.

"His religious differences will not affect my family at all," she said. "Except perhaps to help my children to know that we welcome all people who come in friendship, no matter what their differences. That is what my fadde taught us in his church."

Aunt Zony chuckled in agreement. "That is the answer I expected from you and Jim," she said.

"What about his food?" asked Mama. "We had neighbors who kept kosher when we came to this country. Geneva would know little about that."

"He does not keep kosher, so he can take his meals with my family. We can easily adjust to his diet," said Aunt Zony. "Then I will write to his mother that he is welcome in our homes."

"I would like to have a young man with a fine mind and an education around Jimmy. He will be the family scholar, Zony, I think. Since Geneva says it will be no imposition to cook for one more, it will be our pleasure to have the young man."

"He can take his meals with us, so we can watch his dietary restrictions. Ruth will be helping me all summer," said Aunt Zony. "I don't have a bed on the place that is not filled. He only needs a place to sleep."

"And the money will help James to pay the bills," added Mama. "I know that my doctor bills have strained him. He tries to keep things from me, but he talks to Tarp on the porch and to Bob when he comes home from the north end of the county. I hear. I know Jim's planning to run a pack of hogs over in the cove this summer. They can eat mast, and it won't cost us anything. That will help, I think."

"I think this young Myron Farber could be the answer to your prayers. His father wants him to have some experience working in the out-of-doors, so he could help Jim with the haying, the plowing, and other farmwork, too."

"When will he be coming?" asked Mama.

"The first of May," said Aunt Zony.

"It is welcome he will be," said Mama. Littlejim, listening from his hiding place on the side porch, thought her voice sounded very tired.

Then he wondered who this *Myron* was who would be their guest for the summer. He was not sure he wanted another boy near his own age around. He had always been the only boy on the place and, despite being the constant target of his father's wrath, he rather liked being the *only* boy.

Chapter 9

A FEW WEEKS LATER Littlejim hitched Scott and Swain to Papa's best wagon, the one Bigjim used to carry corn, pumpkins, and other produce to the Piedmont markets, for the ride to the train station in Spruce Pine. Littlejim wished his papa had a new autymobile like Mr. Vance's or a shiny buggy so their visitor from the city would feel at home, but Papa said that a carriage, good only for carrying people, was for show and a waste of money, so they had never owned a buggy. Littlejim had borrowed Aunt Zony's atlas to look up Philadelphia. Photographs in the book showed automobiles everywhere, with only an occasional buggy or carriage, so he knew their visitor would find a farm wagon primitive.

However, the wagon wheels fairly sparkled as the sunlight shone on the metal, and dragonflies alighted to rest as the wheels turned, taking the boy and his sister to the small mining and lumbering town that was so much more exciting than the village of Plumtree. Nell wore her best Sunday dress and bonnet, while Littlejim had his best pants tucked into the tops of his logging boots.

Arriving at the depot early gave Littlejim time to take Nell up the hill to the Topliff Hotel on Upper Street for the treat he had planned for months. Since his job as dust doodler in Uncle Bob's sawmill had gone to the big mills, the boy missed having the dimes he earned each Saturday. However, with summer approaching, Aunt Zony had hired him to tend her long-neglected flower beds, so he had a bit of spending money in his cache behind the chimney chink.

Two summers ago, when he came to town to be photographed as the winner of the essay contest in the *Kansas City Star*, Mr. Greene had invited him to the hotel for the most wonderful food he had ever tasted. It was like eating Mama's cocoa, only better. When the cold chocolate sweetness had first touched his tongue, he knew that ice cream was a treat he wanted to share with those he loved.

At last, thanks to Mr. Myron Farber, he had an opportunity to share the wonderful food with his sister. He wished he could carry some home to Mama, too. But however hard he thought, he had not been able to figure out a way to get it home after a day's journey in the wagon and keep it from melting on the way.

So, after helping Nell into a chair at the white-cloth-covered table, he ordered two dishes of chocolate ice cream, while she stared at the room's high ceilings in amazement. Her brother watched her, amused.

"Do people really live here?" she asked.

"Only travelers," her brother answered knowingly. "Some people stay for as long as a week or two."

"It must cost a lot," she said as she spooned a bit of the cold chocolate into her mouth. She swallowed and smiled at Littlejim.

"Like it?" he asked.

Smiling, she nodded and ate slowly, savoring each spoonful. As Littlejim scraped the last drop from his dish, he saw a tall, distinguished man enter the dining room and wave.

"I thought I saw you as you came up the steps," the man said, sitting beside Nell. "I was in the barbershop getting a shave. How are you, Jimmy?"

"Tolerably well, Mr. Greene. How have you been?" asked Littlejim, reaching out to shake hands, with a smile of pleasure at the sight of a friend.

"Tolerably well, my boy," said the man. "Tolerably well. And who is this pretty lady? Some beauty you are sparking, Jimmy?"

Nell blushed at the man's words.

"No, sir. She is my sister. Say hello to Mr. Greene, Nell," he added.

Mr. Greene smiled at Nell, taking her tiny hand in his big one. "Well, you are a beauty anyway, my pretty Nell. Do you like ice cream?"

Smiling shyly, she nodded and continued to lick her spoon.

"I'm glad I saw you, Jimmy," said Mr. Greene. "I need to talk with your papa. Is he with you today?"

"No, sir," answered the boy. "He sent Nell and me to the depot to pick up our summer visitor from Philadelphia." Littlejim spoke proudly and knowledgeably as he told Mr. Greene about their guest for the summer.

"Sounds like a good idea," said Mr. Greene. "I've been worried about this lumber situation, what with the big companies moving in. How has that affected your papa? And Bob?"

"Uncle Bob closed his sawmill and went to work for the lumber company," said Littlejim. "Papa is making it as best he can, doing whatever work he can find for the team to do. This summer we are running a brood of Violet's pigs in the springhouse cove. We'll take them to market in the fall. We'll make do, Papa says."

"Make do," Mr. Greene mused. "That might be the motto of the mountain people. My papa used to say, 'Make do or do without.' That is the attitude which has helped mountain people survive since our forefathers first settled these hills."

"Did you hear that the *Star* has entered my essay in

a national competition?" asked Littlejim, remembering the good news and his friend's part in that happy day.

The man listened intently as Littlejim told him about the possibility of attending an academy and of his dreams.

"Well, my boy." The man slapped his thigh, then forgetting all about his dignified demeanor, threw his hat into the air in celebration. "That's the best news I've heard lately!" Then he grew quiet. "Before I forget, I have some news for your pa of an uglier sort. I want you to be sure he gets my message. Any mineral speculators been nosing around your farm of late?"

"Mineral speculators?" Littlejim asked, not understanding what the man meant.

"Men offering what seems to be good money to buy something called mineral rights and promising your land will always remain in your hands. They say they only want to buy the rights to the minerals under the land. They say they are taking all the risks because you might not have any minerals under the land. Sounds like a good deal, right?" said Mr. Greene.

"We have minerals under our land, all right," said Littlejim. "Papa says he knows where the Spring House Mine is, and it's on our property line."

"The fabled Spring House Mine, eh?" asked Mr. Greene, chuckling. "Many's a man would give his eye-teeth to find that vein of mica, I'd allow. But if I were you, I'd keep my mouth closed about that knowledge, my boy. In truth, there is no land in this or the surrounding valleys which is not rich in minerals. That's a good reason not to be bamboozled into selling any rights to anything under, on, or over your land."

"Over?" Littlejim asked.

"Who knows? With aeroplanes and airships, who knows? The rights to the air over your land may one day be valuable, too. I take it you've been reading the *Star?*" said Mr. Greene, with a wink. Littlejim nodded. "Well, it is time for the ten o'clock train, my boy. And you have a visitor to greet, little lady," he said, tweaking Nell's cheek as he stood.

With a serious frown, Mr. Greene said, "Tell Jim that I will be up to talk with him one day soon. Tell him I said in this matter not to trust his neighbors either. Some of our local people are so enamored with the almighty dollar that they are willing to cheat neighbors and kin for a cut from outsiders' ill-gotten gains. Can you remember these things, my boy?"

"Yes, sir," promised Littlejim, rising from his chair to shake hands as Mr. Greene prepared to leave.

When Littlejim asked the waiter for the bill, he said, "It's already taken care of."

"But I didn't even say thank you," Littlejim told Nell.

Chapter 10

WALKING OUT TO the platform as the huge black locomotive chugged into the rail yard, Nell covered her ears, but Littlejim grinned. He loved the noise and excitement of the train, although he would never forget the day Scott and Swain had spooked at the train whistle and had run wildly around the town. That day he had been so frightened, but it had been a good day after all. That was the day he had first met Mr. Greene.

Watching the conductor step down and place his stool on the ground for the passengers to alight, Nell asked, "Is that Mr. Farber?" She pointed to a tall, heavy man who was smoking a cigar and dropping ashes into his beard as he stepped down from the train. Hanging a cane with a gold head over his arm, he marched away toward the stores on the far side of the street.

"No," replied her brother. "Mr. Farber is young. Aunt Zony says he is tall and wears glasses."

"Then that must be Mr. Farber," said Nell. "He is wearing glasses."

A tall young man with black curly hair, two or three years older than Littlejim, wearing a brown suit with a belted jacket, stepped down from the passenger car. Placing his satchel on the cinders that covered the yard, he took off his glasses and polished them. Then he placed them back on his nose, looking around as if for someone familiar. Finally, he looked at Littlejim and Nell, waiting for them to respond.

Littlejim remembered his manners. He stepped around Nell and leaned over to offer his hand to the young man.

"You must be Mr. Farber," he said eagerly, smiling in welcome. "We are here to meet you. You will be staying with us. I am Jimmy, known as Littlejim, Houston."

Relief spread over the young man's face as he took Littlejim's hand briefly. "I'm glad you came to meet me," Mr. Farber said. "I feel a bit lost. Where is our taxicab?"

Littlejim took a deep breath to give himself time to think. He tried to answer the question quickly, wanting so much to show the visitor that he was accustomed to taxicabs.

"What's a taxicab?" Nell was standing on tiptoe to whisper in his ear.

"Shh, Nell," said Littlejim under his breath, turning slightly to include her. Then he turned back. "I'm sorry, sir. I don't think we have taxicabs here yet. I've never seen one. I have my papa's wagon. We cleaned it up yesterday just for your visit. It's around back, on the street. Do you have other trunks with you?"

The young man sprinted up the steps to the station platform, taking them two at a time, and stood towering over Littlejim and Nell as he said, "Only one trunk. It should be in the baggage car. I'll ask the conductor." Dropping his satchel at Littlejim's feet, he turned and sprinted down the platform, calling to the conductor.

"He has the biggest eyes I've ever seen!" said Nell breathlessly. "They look like the eyes of the deer in the woods behind the house."

"Nell," warned her brother. "Mama says it's unmannerly to talk about a person's looks. Shh. He might hear you, and he will think you have no manners."

"No," said Nell emphatically. "He has the biggest, *prettiest* eyes I've ever seen!"

"Perhaps his glasses make them appear bigger," explained Littlejim, not wanting to admit that the young man was a fine figure of a man, a handsome fellow, even though he did not look like anyone Littlejim had ever seen. Nell was going on thirteen, and, no doubt, he thought scornfully, like all the other girls on the Creek, would be smitten with the new boy from the city. Even the girl whose green eyes kept appearing in Littlejim's dreams.

Scoffing under his breath as he turned to ask Nell to carry the fellow's small satchel to the wagon, he went to help with the trunk. Nell stood staring in the direction the young man had gone, smiling slightly. Littlejim was disgusted. His little sister was totally smitten with their new visitor. He would have to talk to Mama about this!

"Take Mr. Farber's satchel to the wagon, Nell," he called gruffly, but Nell hardly heard him.

Chapter 11

THE CREAKING OF the wagon and the steady clip-clop of the team's hooves broke the silence as they turned out of the street into the River Road for the long journey home. A bit in awe of his visitor, Littlejim sat silently guiding the horses out. Mr. Farber was also silent, but sitting between them, Nell, who was usually shy in the presence of strangers, chattered like a magpie, pointing out local landmarks as they passed.

"This is Mullein Hill," she said brightly, indicating the road ahead.

"And what on earth is a mullen?" asked the visitor, with only slightly disguised disdain.

"Papa told me the hill was named for the yellow flower that grows there in summertime," explained Nell. "And over there is Biggerstaff Holler."

"And what is a biggerstaff?" the young man asked, laughing. "And what is a holler? Is it like when you people down here call the hogs, you 'holler' at them?"

"No," said Nell sincerely, missing the edge his derisive tone gave to the words. "A Biggerstaff is a member of the Biggerstaff family. They are good people. And a holler is a narrow place, usually the bed of a mountain stream between two ridges."

"You know," Littlejim interrupted. "Like 'the hollows of the earth,' as it says in the Bible. The dictionary says it is 'a low spot between two elevations.' " He loved to peruse Mr. Osk's dictionary when his work was finished, and he had studied the meanings of many words.

"So the mountaineer has memorized the dictionary, eh?" The young man laughed again, his words still holding an undertone of sarcasm. "Well, well, well. And Toynbee wrote that the southern mountaineers are barbarians."

Littlejim bit his tongue. Mama and Papa would be very disappointed in him if he were rude to their guest. He *would* hold his tongue, at least in front of his sister.

But Nell looked perplexed. "Philadelphia is in Pennsylvania, isn't it?" She continued, not waiting for an answer, but sorting things out aloud. "And Pennsylvania is in the United States, isn't it?" She went on without a pause in her voice. "And people all over the United States speak English, don't they? And they understand English, don't they?"

"What is your meaning, Miss Nell?" asked Mr. Farber.

Her face registered her disappointment. "Then what I don't understand," she said softly, "is why *you* don't understand what I am saying to you. And I don't understand why you are laughing at me when I am trying to be kind to you. I am trying to make you feel welcome, you being so far from home and all."

Littlejim was amazed at his sister's skills of persuasion. He found it hard to believe she was only twelve going on thirteen. She had gently pointed out the man's rudeness and had implied that such behavior was unbecoming from a welcome guest. Being smitten with his brown eyes had not muddled his sister's brain one bit, Littlejim thought, turning to hide a smug grin. Nell had earned a new respect from her brother.

Out of the corner of his eye, Littlejim could see that Mr. Farber's face had turned red as he wiggled uncomfortably and pulled his necktie to loosen it as he began to whistle a tune softly.

Nell sat straight, staring ahead, her chin lifted. The trio rode on in silence, with Littlejim tipping his cap and inquiring about the health of or commenting on the weather to each person they met riding in another vehicle or walking along the road.

" 'Tolerably well'?" Mr. Farber said finally, an edge returning to his voice. "What on earth does that mean? As Miss Nell pointed out, I thought I spoke the king's English. Apparently I was wrong! And the pronunciations! What does it mean when a man answers your question about his health with the statement that he is 'plumb tarred out'?"

Wondering if he would spend his summer explaining

his world to this young man who was a university student, Littlejim said, "*Tolerably well* means the person is in generally good health. And *tarred* is the way most folks here say *t-i-r-e-d*."

"Ha," said the young man, almost snorting.

"Stop, Littlejim!" commanded Nell, her voice choked as she scrambled across Littlejim's legs and stepped on the wagon spoke to climb to the ground. As she ran toward a rhododendron thicket on the embankment near the river, Littlejim fixed the reins and jumped down behind his sister.

"What's wrong?" Littlejim asked, but Nell pushed him away. "What can I do to help you?"

"You can put that rude man back on the train!" she said between sobs. "He doesn't belong here. He laughs at us. Send him back to Philadelphia where people speak to suit him until he can see that a person is trying to make him feel welcome."

Littlejim grabbed his sister in a fierce hug, but she fought him until he locked his arms around her and held her head against his chest, allowing her to sob. No matter how angry he was at their guest, he felt his first duty was to comfort his sister and to help calm her. Besides, he needed time to think over the situation, to decide how to handle this rude young man so his family did not have to suffer him for the whole summer.

As the pair walked back to the wagon, Littlejim could see Myron Farber spinning his cap around and around on his finger while looking at the sky as if the answer to some important question might be written there.

"If you don't mind, I would appreciate your moving to the bed of the wagon to sit. My sister is not feeling well," said Littlejim to Myron, speaking as sternly as he could.

"No," said Nell, walking around to the tailgate of the wagon. "I will sit on the gate, so I can lie down if I need to."

Littlejim unfastened the tailgate and helped her up to sit on the back edge of the wagon bed. As he climbed into the driver's seat, he looked at Mr. Farber with narrowed eyes, and with his jaw firmly set he spoke quietly. "Mr. Farber, you have made my sister feel very bad. She was trying to be kind, but you met her efforts with ridicule. I think you owe her an apology, don't you?"

The two young men sat for a moment, not more than a foot apart, staring into each other's eyes, as Littlejim wondered if this was the way all educated people from big cities behaved. Accustomed as he was to the courtesy of the people he knew, Littlejim found it difficult to understand how a guest could display such disrespectful behavior to people who welcomed him. For the first time, he questioned his dream of going to the city to study and perhaps to live. If this was an example of educated behavior, he was not sure he wanted to be *educated* like Mr. Farber.

Littlejim's thoughts were interrupted as Mr. Farber said sarcastically, "My father thought a summer among these ignorant mountaineers would make a man of me. So I must begin the process by apologizing to a girl!" The two young men continued to stare at one another, faces inches apart, but Littlejim was thinking, So, there are fathers like mine in other places, even in Philadelphia!

Chapter 12

THEIR GUEST'S WORDS about his father in Philadelphia continued to haunt Littlejim's thoughts each day as he mended fences and took care of other summer chores around the farm. He and Nell rarely saw their guest. He left the adjoining room in the sleeping loft before Aunt Geneva called them down to breakfast, took his meals at Aunt Zony's house, and climbed the narrow stairs after they had blown out their lamps to prepare for sleep.

"I don't care if I don't see him all summer," said Nell, still angry at their guest. "As rude as he is, he can just stay in Philadelphia where he belongs!"

Myron spent most of his days working with Uncle Pierce, who built houses and barns, and his evenings in conversation with Aunt Zony. His aunt had invited Littlejim to join them, but he did not want to compete with a college student for her attention, so he declined. Occasionally, when Bigjim needed another man in the woods, their guest joined the logger for the day. He had avoided Littlejim and Nell since their ride home from the train station. Sometimes after supper he would return to join Bigjim on the porch to talk about the timber situation, but whenever Littlejim joined them, he excused himself, saying he had letters to write.

As the days of June passed, the weather grew warmer. Soon it was time to cut the first crop of hay from the meadow in the bottomland near the creek. That would be followed by the haying in the meadow uphill from the barn, and finally the cutting of the steep meadow far across the creek near the family cemetery, where members of the family had been buried since the time before the War Between the States.

Although the work was hard, hot, and tiring, Littlejim liked haying time. It was exciting to work under the racing morning clouds gathering across the Spear Tops to stack the hay before afternoon showers could wet the precious crop, causing it to mold and rot in the stack. If the workers won the race, the cattle, horses, and oxen would eat bountifully next winter. Feeding their livestock through the winter was a crucial issue on the Creek, Littlejim knew. If the hay crop was good, hard money used to purchase feed in lean years could be saved or spent for human needs and extras such as white sugar and cocoa.

All the residents of the Creek community helped one another at haying time. Equipment such as mowing machines and rakes was owned by the farmers who owned the most land, so it had to be scheduled for loan to each neighbor in return for labor or a portion of the crop. Everyone worked together haying on each farm. The women and girls joined forces to cook and serve huge midday dinners. Gardens were just coming in, and the meals were as much a celebration of the first harvest of fresh vegetables as they were sustenance for hardworking bodies.

Haying time took on the air of a festival involving everyone in the community. The camaraderie of working together toward a common goal, the smell of new-mown hay and the fragrance of huge black pots of vegetables, the pride in work well done, all were part of the feeling each person felt in the community effort. Littlejim took special pleasure in the feeling of responsibility his assigned post as topper for the haystacks gave him. Each year since he was ten, Papa had assigned him to do the important work of carefully stacking each mound of hay so that the top formed a layer that water could not penetrate. Doing this work carefully assured that the hay would be good food for the animals in winter.

Most of all he enjoyed the end of each day, when the younger men raced, even though their muscles screamed with exhaustion, to the rocks that formed a pool in the Creek. The cold water was deep enough that they could jump into its chilly depths and, with cakes of lye soap made by the women in each family, wash the dust and grime of haying from their sun-blistered skin. Even Bigjim, usually taciturn, seemed to enjoy slipping his overalls and shirt from his skinny frame and throwing off his heavy logging boots to join his neighbors in the pool formed by a layer of stone arranged by rainstorms in a time long past memory.

This year things changed. Instead of his assigning him to top the haystacks, his father told Littlejim to join the men who gleaned the hay left by the horse-drawn rakes so none would be wasted. "Awkwardness" was his only comment as he left his son humiliated in front of the men of the community. "You don't belong on that haystack." And abruptly Bigjim climbed back on the hay rake to ride to the far end of the field.

Young Farber, standing nearby, stood looking at Littlejim across the width of the hay wagon. As Bigjim rode away, the young man's eyes met Littlejim's for a moment, sympathetically ready to say something. Then he turned to follow the rake. Littlejim remembered the words their guest had said that day on the way from the railroad station. Did that father, so far away in the big city of Philadelphia, think his son was "not much of a man" either?

Littlejim compared his own skinny frame, with his long legs that looked to him like sticks, to the well-developed muscles of the young man from the city. His spirits fell. If their summer guest was not much of a man, Littlejim thought he never would achieve the status of manhood.

Stopping under a darkening sky to rest and fan his steaming face with his wide straw hat, Littlejim watched the men working, sweat staining their rugged shirts, all except Mr. Farber. In the heavy heat and humidity, he had shed his shirt, something a mountain boy would never have done, and the muscles in his back, now browned from days in the sun, rippled in a manly way as he lifted the hay. Littlejim had never hated anyone before, but he was sure that what he felt toward their summer visitor was hatred. The young man was so perfect, so manly. Surely any father would be proud to have such a son, and one with a university education to boot. How he wished Myron Farber had stayed in Philadelphia where, as Nell said, he belonged. He did *not* belong on Henson Creek, where Littlejim could be compared to him!

Littlejim's anger came in waves until a roaring noise in the distance slowly made its way into his thoughts. The sound grew louder and louder. Shading his eyes with one hand, Littlejim turned to face the far cove in back of the Houston house where the mountain met the sky, to see a black dot grow larger and larger until it took on the shape of a dragonfly. He forgot his anger as he realized that he was watching a flying machine making its way through the sky over his papa's farm.

"Look! Look!" he called, running across the stubbled grass toward his father, who had stopped the team and rake to gaze at the sky. "It's a flying machine!" Almost falling over the wheel of the hay rake, he realized that each man in the hay field had stopped, as if frozen in the hot, humid sunlight, to watch the aeroplane dip one wing in greeting, circle once overhead, and climb away from the thunderclouds gathering in the west. Then it disappeared.

Closing his eyes to savor a small breeze, Littlejim, in his mind, soared away with the flying machine, dipping and gliding across the sky, on his way to adventures he could only imagine, adventures that lay on the other side of the mountain. With the hot sun beating down on his bare head, he lifted his face toward the western sky and smiled. One day, he knew he would fly in a real airship!

Just then he was startled to hear a voice close to his side, the words pronounced in an unfamiliar way. "Never seen a flying machine before, eh, country boy? Bunch of yokels here, staring at an aeroplane like it's some kind of miracle! Well, it's no miracle. I rode one last year at the Exhibition. Pity you never will, here in this back-water place," the voice said, a sharp edge honing its sarcastic tone.

Littlejim, normally the most gentle boy on the Creek, felt his anger at and jealousy of the intruder into his world rise from a place deep within himself and find its way to his hands. Flinging the rake to the ground, he caught Myron under the chin with his fist, catching him off guard and throwing him back to land on the bristling stalks of newly cut grass, his glasses flying through the air to land on his knee.

For a moment, Littlejim was confused by the power of his own anger toward the young man and by his amusement at the startled expression on their guest's face. He had never realized it could feel so good to let all that energy out through his fist. Then, turning contrite, he reached out his hand to help Myron to his feet. But Myron, catching him off guard, pulled him forward. Littlejim went sprawling on the ground, the sharp stalks of grass cutting his face as he felt the weight of a larger body on his back.

"What on earth is going on here?" Struggling to turn over, Littlejim heard his father's voice as the weight was lifted from his shoulders. A hand grasped his arm and pulled him to a standing position, to look into his father's angry face. His first thought was that he had not realized that he was almost as tall as his papa. Then Bigjim said, "This is no time for a fight! Don't you see that sky? The rain is going to beat us in this field. We will settle this later, back at the house. Now get back to work."

Littlejim and Myron glowered at each other for a few seconds, then each boy picked up his hay fork and began to work. His anger and embarrassment fueling his energy, Littlejim's muscles powered his hands and arms as he focused on his anger and the hay on the ground in front of him. Never had he worked so hard in his whole life. As the stacks were topped and the last forkful of hay was loaded on the wagon to be stored in the

DATE DUE

FEB 0 3 20			
MAY 1 4 '19			

#47-0108 Peel Off Pressure Sensitive

DATE DUE

barn, the sky opened up to pour buckets of rain down on the haying workers.

Littlejim walked slowly, holding his face up to allow the rain to cool it. As his hair and clothing became soaked, he felt some of his anger wash away with the rain. But a large part of that anger was stored in a place in his heart for the future, when he could say just how he felt to their visitor. He would find a way to make their visitor feel as bad as he had felt just before the storm!

Chapter 13

T HE FOLLOWING DAY, it rained, not a soft summer rain but a hard, cold, driving rain, chilling body and soul as it fell on skin so newly sunburned in the hayfields. Littlejim spent the morning mending harness and cleaning the horses' stables.

As he lifted a shovelful of muck from Scott's stable, a voice said from outside the wall, "Do you have another shovel? I'll give you a hand."

The last person on earth Littlejim wanted to join him was their summer guest, but he had promised his papa the previous evening that he would show courtesy and attempt to hide his animosity.

"Hanging on the wall beside the shed," Littlejim replied to Myron, with a jerk of his head in the direction of the tools. "Only Swain's to go," said Littlejim, his expression questioning whether Myron meant his words.

"Then let's get it done," said Myron. "Miserable day, isn't it?"

"A day like this is a welcome pleasure in the summertime," said Littlejim, not wanting to agree with anything his guest said. "Too wet to do much outside work. When the barn chores are done, I can read for a few hours until time for evening chores. That pleasures me."

Stopping to lean on the handle of the shovel, Myron smiled. "What does it *pleasure* you to read, Jimmy?"

Stopping to lean against the door of the stall to allow him to consider whether Myron's interest in what he read was genuine, Littlejim waited for a moment before he spoke. Actually, helping Papa and Aunt Geneva since Mama's illness had left him little time to read in recent days, a situation he was not ready to reveal to their guest, so he finally said, "I have a book by Jules Verne I'm reading for the third time, but it gets better with each reading. I had hoped to get back to it this afternoon. And most folks hereabouts, except Mama, call me *Littlejim*."

"All right, Littlejim," said Myron, working to keep up with his younger partner. "Now that you can stand eyeball to eyeball with your father, what shall we call you?"

Littlejim smiled. It had been a surprise yesterday when he realized that he had grown to be as tall as his father. "Still Littlejim, I guess," he said. "Until I am the man my father is."

"From the power of your fist yesterday, I'd say you

are," said Myron, rubbing his chin and moving it side to side.

"I am sorry that I hit you," said Littlejim, embarrassed both by Myron's compliment and the reference to the fight. "Mama would be disappointed in me, but I was so angry with you and with Papa. I do not hit people." He hesitated. "Usually, that is."

"I would have been angry with your papa, too," said Myron. "I think he meant to protect you from falling off the haystack. Your arms and legs have recently grown so much that you do not have the coordination you will acquire in a few more months. He handled the situation badly, so that you were humiliated. He behaved very much like my father behaves sometimes. He scolds me so often that I sometimes feel that nothing I do pleases him."

Littlejim had often wondered if his guest had the same problems with his father in the city that he suffered with Bigjim. "I know," he said, nodding his head sympathetically. "No matter how hard I try, nothing pleases him. And yesterday, he took away my job as the topper, as if I could not do that either."

"I think that you have grown very fast. I had that experience a couple of years ago. The doctor explained it to me as a *growth spurt*. When I fell and broke my wrist, I had to learn to move all over again. You will have to re-learn also," said Myron. "Your father has observed you stumbling. He doesn't want you to get hurt. This is not the year for you to top the hay-stacks."

Littlejim was considering all that his guest had told him when he was startled to have his guest slap him on the shoulder in comradeship, so startled that he managed only to stammer, "Much, uh, much obliged, Mr. Farber."

"And my name is *Myron,*" he told Littlejim. "After working side by side in the hay fields, don't you think 'Mr. Farber' is a bit formal, Littlejim? Especially when we both have *fathers?*" He emphasized the word with a resigned shrug. "Now, what were you telling me about Jules Verne's books? He is one of my favorite authors, too."

"I like to think about whether the things in his books could possibly happen," said Littlejim. "I like to ask, 'What if...?'" Littlejim smiled and began to shovel muck again.

"I like his books, too," said Myron. "But my father finds all fiction a waste of time. I am supposed to read only serious things which will," he sneered, quoting what Littlejim assumed to be his Philadelphia father's vocal inflections, "*enrich my mind and aid me in having an outstanding legal career.* Ha!"

"Your papa tells you what to read?" asked Littlejim. "My papa never seems to notice what I am reading unless I have his *Kansas City Star,* and it is missing from the mantel when he is ready to read it. Why would your father care what you read?"

The two young men stopped their work and looked at each other, recognizing a commonality between them. With a move as if a team had been established, they began their work again in one motion, reminding Littlejim of the tandem movements made by Scott and Swain when they pulled the wagon.

"I guess we each have a difficult time pleasing that important and all-wise father in our lives, don't we?" asked Myron, a bit embarrassed to admit their common plight.

"I don't think I've ever done anything my papa was pleased with in my life, except perhaps to have my essay printed in the *Star*," said Littlejim.

"Mrs. Zona was telling me about that," said Myron. "Tell me more."

As they cleared the dirt floor of the stable together and hauled the muck to the pile at the edge of the field near Mama's vegetable garden, Littlejim told Myron about the events involved in writing the essay, the day at the picnic when he read his work to celebrate July Fourth, and the trip to town to have his photograph made and taste ice cream for the first time.

"That is quite an accomplishment," said Myron. "You mountaineers are a great deal more intelligent than I realized. I mean, based on what I read and heard before

I came down here. Perhaps Toynbee was wrong, eh?"
Myron watched to make sure Littlejim knew he was teas-
ing with his last statement.

"Mr. Osk says that we know a great deal about other
people and places, but outsiders don't know very much
about us. He says that most people who visit us only
look at the ways in which we are different and do not
take the time to get to know us," said Littlejim, emp-
tying the wheelbarrow and cleaning it with his shovel.
When he beat his shovel against the ground to clean it,
Myron followed his example.

"Of course, Mother told us about Mrs. Zona, but I
thought she was quite the exception," said Myron. "I
have been impressed by the general intelligence of the
population here. Nobody is what I expected to find, especially your father. He is really an intelligent man, al-
beit uneducated. I have enjoyed our conversations."

"Papa had to leave school early to help his family,"
said Littlejim. "He hardly learned to read. Mama says
that he takes great pride in his acquaintance with the
world by reading the *Star*."

"Education and intelligence are not the same
thing," said Myron. "My mother is fond of telling us
that—over and over—when we act as if we are superior
just because my family has had privileges others have
not enjoyed. We who live in large cities with schools and
universities available do not realize how fortunate we are

to have the opportunities to develop our natural abilities. If your father had been born in Philadelphia, as intelligent as he is, he would have found a way to get an education. Those opportunities are simply not available here."

"Yes, you are fortunate," said Littlejim. "When I was little, my greatest dream was to be a logger with a team like my papa, but now I hope to go away to school. I would like to be a teacher or…" He stopped, a bit embarrassed. "An aviator."

"I don't know why you shouldn't do either one if you like, Littlejim. Seems to me you could do anything you want," said Myron. "It's a great pity more educational opportunities are not available to you here."

Littlejim could not resist a bit of sarcasm. "So we could learn to pronounce our words more like people who live in Philadelphia? And so people don't have to explain what a 'holler' is," he said, with an edge to his voice denied by the smile on his face, but watching for his guest's reaction.

"Oh, that," said Myron. It was his turn to be embarrassed. "That is a long story. I hated coming here for the summer. My father made me come, because, as he said, the *hard work and deprivation of the backwoods* would turn me into a man. You and Nell were handy targets for my anger at my father, I guess."

"Our idea of courtesy may not fit the one you know,

but people who live here usually think of the feelings of others before they speak. We think it unmannerly not to think of others," said Littlejim.

"Yes, Littlejim," said Myron. "I have traveled extensively with my parents. I have found the people here to be as courteous as any I have ever met. I did not expect to find that here. I had read that mountain people were very wild and primitive."

"And we are?" Littlejim chuckled, but waited anxiously for the answer.

"Hardly, except in hay fields," Myron said with a wry grin. "A woman as well-read as Mrs. Zona, as sweet and kind as your mother and Miss Geneva, a man as knowledgeable about the effects of national politics on the local scene as your father, a writer who competes nationally who is younger than I am—I did not expect to meet any of these in the mountains. And now I meet someone else who likes Jules Verne's books, too," said Myron with an unbelieving shake of his head.

"*So* we aren't *too* bad," said Littlejim with a grin. The rain had stopped, and the clouds had parted to allow beams of sunlight, which warmed their shoulders and brightened their spirits as they left the barnyard.

"You aren't bad at all," said Myron. "I have been made to feel very welcome. The people here are very like those in my family and my synagogue. Your social lives revolve around your church. Your families and communities are close-knit. You help and support each other. You have fewer modern amusements and less money than we have in Philadelphia, but you have a pleasant life. I like it here."

The two boys stood awkwardly for a few moments, neither knowing quite what to say.

Then Myron broke the silence. "I would like for us to be friends, Littlejim," he said, offering his hand. "I think we have a lot in common."

Littlejim's grin widened as he shook Myron's hand.

"Fathers!" they said in one voice.

Chapter 14

GOOD THING Violet's litter this spring was a big one," Littlejim heard his father tell Myron as they sat on the front porch next day watching the rain fall slowly through the mist that shrouded the yard.

"Are you going to keep all of them?" asked Myron. "Will you have enough corn to feed them over the winter?"

Littlejim looked up from the article he was reading in the *Star* to listen more carefully to his father's plans and shifted into a more comfortable position as he leaned against the supporting column of the front porch. Whatever his father planned to do would affect his hopes of going away to school. He felt restless inside, wondering if a time would ever come that his family would not need him, a time when he could be free to follow the path to his own dreams. He remembered Mama's words that life without dreams has no direction. Sometimes this summer he had felt that his life had no direction, no dreams, but he knew that as the eldest child, his family must, for the present at least, *must* come before his own wishes. Each time he thought of Mama lying just inside the door, his heart felt like the rain slowly falling off the roof, soft and sad.

"Well." His father's voice intruded on his thoughts. "In times past, when my grandsire homesteaded on this Creek, folks had fences around their kitchen gardens and their corn patches to keep the animals out. Livestock was allowed to forage in the woods and medders. Hogs would grow fat on mast they found in the fall of the year. A man could grow two herds ready for market every year, if he was a mind to."

"So fences were used to keep livestock out, not to keep them in as they are today?" said Myron. "What a novel idea."

"Except for the land right around a man's house, any land not under cultivation was considered common land. A feller took what he needed and left some for the next man who needed it. Hogs and cattle ran wild, only to be rounded up for market or butchering," Bigjim told them.

"Sounds a lot like the way the cattle ranchers did it out west until the invention of barbed wire," said Myron. "That takes a lot of cooperation between neighbors. How did you know which animals were yours when you rounded them up?"

"Cattle you branded, just like out west," said Bigjim.

"Hogs you marked by a notch in their ears. Back then, every farmer had a notch of a different design." Bigjim continued. "Sometimes disagreements happened. Once in a while two fellers would have a falling-out over the pattern of notches in a sow's ear, and things got right unpleasant. Now, bob-war fences and new laws changed all that too."

"You mean there *were* feuds like the Hatfields and McCoys, with Old Devil Anse and his bunch," said Myron with a chuckle. "I always thought those stories to be more fiction than reality. Did they really happen here?"

"Not in many years, not in this area," replied Bigjim, taking out his pocketknife and a piece of soft pine, rearranging his chair to lean against the porch railing, and beginning to whittle.

Littlejim lay down the *Star*. Whittling was something he rarely saw his father do, and it usually meant he was thinking deeply about something.

"The newspapers made a lot out of that feud. Feuds are pretty much a thing of the past," said Bigjim. "Most folks, leastways around here, are willing to let a court of law settle their disagreements these days. Feuds are left over from our grandsires and the ways of the clans they brought from the old country. Land and forage were so scarce over there, and what with the gentry controlling the best of the grazing land and all, families had to band together to take the best land available, or they would have starved. Most of the old ways have changed in my lifetime. Makes for a lot less bloodshed."

Littlejim wondered if he had heard his papa correctly. Perhaps his papa was changing, too. Littlejim chuckled. It was more than he had dared to hope!

Then he heard Myron say, "Before I came down here, my friends at the university warned me that a travel writer from *Scribner's Magazine* called this region lawless and violent. Something about a feud over some mica mines, I believe, somewhere around Spruce Pine. Others reminded me that Toynbee wrote that mountaineers were degenerate and barbaric. I've yet to see any evidence of these things here."

"We used to have some of the same violence around here over mineral rights thirty or forty years ago that miners had in the big strikes out west, or so Galen tells me. Somehow, though, the men who wrote about those disputes found them noble and exciting, while the ones who wrote about these parts found them violent and barbaric. Never did understand the difference myself. Galen and me, we've chewed on that for many a day. Still don't understand it." Bigjim shook his head and continued his carving.

"Have you ever read the magazine articles about the people who live here? Do local people realize how they are viewed by the outside world?" asked Myron.

"I guess most of us are too busy living to think much about what the rest of the world thinks, unless somebody reminds us about it," said Bigjim. He was silent for a few moments, focused on the movement of his knife and the shape forming from the wood in his hands. "I remember hearing about that article, though, written by a man by the name of Warner, as I recall. I think he wrote a book about his visit here, too. Made a lot of people around here mad, so I heard," said Bigjim. "Both were written about the time I was born. It seems that when something gets written down, people always think it is true, even when it has disappeared. Too bad that people off from here still believe that about us."

Littlejim wondered how anybody could believe that a place had not changed in thirty or forty years. Why, he thought, that was his papa's whole lifetime!

"My father was a bit worried about my safety here, but then my mother said she would find it difficult to believe that such a refined person as Mrs. Zona came from a culture of lawlessness and violence. So she urged me to come for the summer," said Myron. "My father thought it would make a man of me."

Bigjim could not see the glance Littlejim gave him as he heard his father say, "All that belongs to a time past. But I guess some people need to keep it alive, long after it's outlived its usefulness."

"I guess we humans keep a lot of things alive long after they have outlived their usefulness," said Myron, speaking slowly, as if his mind were on something else. "Like not allowing women to vote, I guess."

"All that's going to change now since that new Nineteenth Amendment is likely to pass Congress," said Bigjim with a shrug. "Women can think and vote as good as any man. Look at Zony. She's a match for any man. She's a magistrate here, you know. And I've seen a lot of men who hadn't sense enough to vote."

"So you think keeping the vote to ourselves is a practice left over from the past that's outlived its time?" asked Myron with a laugh. "We like to hang on to things whether they have a purpose or not, don't we?"

"Seems as if we do," mused Bigjim, still carving, his knife slowly shaping the tiny piece of wood into the rough shape of a bird. "Like all this talk about keeping Germany down since the war. The war is over. We may as well let those poor people go back to living their lives instead of punishing them for something their leaders caused."

"I see you read the editorial in the *Star* today," said Myron. "Do you think President Wilson is right, that the League of Nations will make the Great War one to end all wars?"

"It seems to me that treaty signed over there in France a few weeks ago was mite harsh on the Germans. We whupped them. Seems to me that's enough. When a fight's over, it ought to be over and finished," said Bigjim. "You keep on whipping a dog, it just gets meaner. Seems to me the same would be true of a country. Or a people."

"I think Europe has lost so much of its population,

with the war and the influenza epidemic, that there's no country there with enough men to fight again," said Myron. "I guess that means our nation is the champion nation for a while."

"Just like Jack Dempsey," said Littlejim, eager to talk about the prizefighter he had been reading about in the *Star* before his father and Myron had joined him. "After he knocked out Jess Willard last year, I think he'll be a champion for a long time."

"He'll be champion until another man knocks *him* out," said Bigjim disdainfully, and returned to his conversation with Myron. "We were lucky here on the Creek. We only had a few cases of that flu. Heard it was a bad one, though. Killed more people than the guns of the Great War. Glad to see them both end."

"The end of the war hurt the market for timber here on the Creek, though, didn't it?" asked Myron.

"Might nigh as much as the big timber companies hurt it. Brother Bob's quest for the almighty dollar hurt my prospects about as much as anything. Closing his mill left no place for me or the other loggers here to get our timber milled into boards so we can sell it at market. Brothers don't leave brothers, or neighbors, to fend for themselves, unless they have to. Families stick together and work together."

"Is that attitude still a holdover from the herders in the old country, do you think?" asked Myron. "When one's survival depended on the cooperation and support of the entire group?"

Bigjim harrumphed his contempt for such wool-gathering. "Blood's thicker than water," was his answer.

Littlejim sat thinking about what Myron had said. So many things made sense when he thought of them as being parts of the way of life from the olden days, kept into his own lifetime, little changed from the time when his great-grandfather had come over from Scotland in the days of Jefferson's presidency. Maybe, he thought, that was the reason the ways of the folks who lived on the Creek seemed strange to outsiders. They were simply different from the ways of people who lived in Philadelphia.

Then he wondered if the ways of the people here were so different from the ways people in Philadelphia had lived in the past. One day soon he would get his chance to ask Myron about those things. A person who has studied history at a university should be able to answer such questions, or so Littlejim thought.

"I wonder if Littlejim could accompany me to the railway station on Monday?" Myron asked Bigjim. "One of my father's clients is a travel writer for *Harper's Monthly Magazine*. He is traveling through the South looking for some local color stories. My father showed him my letters describing the people here, and he wants to visit here to do some articles."

"Jimmy has to drive the hogs up to the top of the ridge to change their feeding grounds. And the corn needs hoeing one more time," said Bigjim. "If he gets that work done, he will be free to go with you." Turning to Littlejim, he added, "Mind you he behaves himself like a gentleman in front of visitors from the big city."

"As if I had not gone to the station alone already," whispered Littlejim under his breath. "And as if Myron weren't from the big city!"

His father blew on his carving, now a tiny bird in flight, handed it to his very surprised guest, cleaned his pocketknife, and returned it to its usual storage place in the pocket of his overalls. Then he picked up his newspaper and folded it under his arm.

Littlejim and Myron both sat staring at the tiny bird resting on Myron's hand until Bigjim's voice startled them. "Mind you behave like a gentleman, son," his father said quietly as he entered the house.

"I'll help you with your duties. But how are we going to drive the hogs to the cove? They are so big we can only get one or two into the wagon for each trip. That will take days!" said Myron.

Laughing heartily, Littlejim said, "We don't take them in the wagon! We drive cattle and hogs by herding them on foot or on horseback. We stay behind them to keep them moving, making a lot of noise and rounding up strays."

"Oh, that kind of drive," said Myron, joining in the laughter. "Like the cattle drive I saw on a ranch in Montana summer before last," said Myron, jumping up to run into the yard. "Ya-hoo!" he shouted, pretending to throw his imaginary hat into the air, then to swing a rope to catch an imaginary animal.

Littlejim jumped up and joined in the fun, riding an imaginary horse down the steps, a bucking bronco that leaped and dived while he fought to stay on its back, shouting with every move. Myron was busy pretending to drive an imaginary herd forward, shouting to them to move on. Littlejim swung his imaginary rope to capture one of the herd, both boys jumping and yelling.

As they fell to the ground shouting with laughter, Bigjim came through the door to say, "Can you keep that infernal racket down out here! You're loud enough to wake the dead!"

But Littlejim thought he saw a hint of a smile curving his father's mustache.

Chapter 15

LITTLEJIM AND MYRON were so excited that they arrived two hours early at the railway station. The
bustle and excitement made Littlejim's head swim as he
watched passengers gathering and goods being made
ready for the arriving train. Still he could hardly pull
himself away from the new Jules Verne book Myron had
loaned him. From time to time the sounds of the busy
town intruded, and he would stop to watch the loafers,
as the town residents called those who rode into town
to spend all day Saturday visiting with one another, discussing local politics and swapping tales. He wished he
could come every Saturday, but his father had made his
opinion clear about those who came "to see and be
seen." Those who had nothing better to do with their
time were the only people for whom Bigjim had little
respect.

Myron was stretched across the wagon bed, his arms
folded behind his head, his broad-brimmed hat, newly

acquired at Burleson's Store to make him look more like a native, pushed down to shade his eyes. Tilting the brim of the hat up slightly, Myron asked, "Who are those people?" He was pointing to a poorly dressed group making its way toward the depot.

A tall man with a long beard walked in front. A few feet behind him walked a small woman, her back bent, carrying a baby and clutching a toddler by the hand. In a row behind the pair, several children walked single file, their heights decreasing like stair steps. All the members of the group looked poorly fed and sickly. They were all barefoot, even the parents.

"They're 'sangers," said Littlejim. "Come to town for their Saturday outing. Live way back in the hollers, probably from around Mallow town."

"Singers?" said Myron, sitting up straight and looking intently at the group. "What do they sing? They look too starved to sing."

Littlejim smiled at the misunderstanding. " 'Sangers," he explained. "Ginseng. We call it ' 'sang.' It is a wild plant, grows in the deep coves and hollers of the mountains, up where those people probably live. They make their living digging 'sang and other yarbs"—he stopped and corrected himself—"herbs. Most of their land is too steep and poor to grow anything but a scrubby patch of corn now and then. They have a hard life."

This time Myron rushed to put his friend at ease.

"Mrs. Zona has already added *yarbs* to my vocabulary."

"The 'sangers stay off by themselves, guarding the knowledge of their 'sang beds jealously. Some of them make moonshine out of their corn crop. They just don't fit into places like the Creek or into the town."

"They're the outsiders, the rebels. They treasure their independence. They have no desire to come into the modern world with the rest of us," said Myron. "I read an article a few years ago in *Harper's Monthly* about a group of mountain people the writer called 'Hill-Billies.' I'm glad to finally see some of them. When I came here I expected everyone to be like those people. I was disappointed that you did not live in a shack and make moonshine in a still in the holler." He grinned at Littlejim, watching the effect of the word on his friend. "I was surprised when you weren't what the travel writers had described."

"Did you really expect us to be like those people?" asked Littlejim. "Is that the reason you were so unkind at first?"

"You won't let me forget that, will you?" said Myron. "Yes, I suppose so. I would have found it difficult to fit into that group. For instance, I have been taught to respect all people equally—men and women."

Climbing back to sit on the wagon bed, Littlejim watched the eldest daughter of the 'sanger family open a basket to offer her father food first, then offer it to her brothers and finally to her mother and sisters. Quietly, the family began to eat.

"And we think we have troubles with our fathers," mused Myron. "How would you like to be that old man's son?"

"I would rather be his son than his daughter," replied Littlejim. "If food were short, I expect his daughters would go hungry."

"It looks that way," Myron replied, shaking his head in disbelief.

Littlejim tried to remember how Mama had explained the differences in the people who lived back in the hollers to him. "Their ways are different. They are good people, but they have different beliefs and customs," she had told him. "We should never disrespect them because they are different. They do all they know."

"It's amazing," said Myron. "There are as many different cultures in this small area as there are in Philadelphia, and no two of them are alike."

"Do you have poor people like the 'sangers in Philadelphia?" asked Littlejim.

Myron thought for a moment. "I guess so. I read about things that happen in the newspaper. Sometimes I see them if we go into the poor part of the city, but generally they live so far away from us that we don't realize they are there. Here it seems that people, whether poor or not poor—I haven't seen any rich people here—all seem to be all mixed up. In the city we are more separated."

Each time they talked, Littlejim took away many new

ideas to think about. He had only traveled as far as the next county, so he had learned much from their guest. He was very happy Aunt Zony had arranged for their summer together.

"Do you have the paper with your essay in it?" asked Myron. "I want Mr. Bradley to be impressed with your writing."

"Right here," Littlejim said, pulling a package wrapped in newspaper from underneath the wagon seat. "Wrapped. In case it rains again today," he explained, not wanting to tell Myron that each time he thought about meeting a real writer from a real magazine, his hands grew sweaty, and he was afraid he might smear the ink.

"Good idea," said Myron. They heard the train's whistle blowing as the train rounded the curve into the station. Climbing down from the wagon, they walked across the station platform to wait for their visitor. As soon as the conductor placed his step on the ground, a short, stocky man stepped down from the train, dressed very much as Myron had been that first day, carrying a leather valise. A pocket full of pencils marked him as different from the others. He was followed by a man in a wildly colored plaid coat who had leather bags hanging from his shoulders and arms and who carried a tripod over his shoulder.

The short man moved so quickly along the siding that Myron had to hurry to catch up and shake his hand.

Littlejim stumbled on the gravel, almost falling against the locomotive's giant wheels.

"Mr. Bradley," Myron shouted over the noise. "Meet Littlejim Houston. Bennington Bradley, travel writer for several fine publications. Mr. Bradley, my North Carolina friend, Jimmy Houston, better known as Littlejim."

Shaking hands with the man, Littlejim realized that the man was no taller than his shoulder. He was surprised by the man's stature. Somehow he had expected a real journalist who wrote for national magazines and newspapers to be larger than other men.

Looking up, the man commented, "Little Jim. Doesn't look so little to me."

"Littlejim," explained Myron. "As opposed to Bigjim, his father."

"Your father must be a big man, son," said the writer, chuckling. He spoke so fast that Littlejim had the feeling that his ears were running to catch up with the man's words. "Meet my photographer, Wiley Schmidt. Wiley, you may want to set up your cameras on the platform. Shoot a bit of local color, if you will."

"Littlejim is a writer, too. He won the top prize in an essay competition in the *Kansas City Star* and is now in a national competition for a scholarship," said Myron proudly, placing a hand on Littlejim's shoulder to propel him forward.

Mr. Bradley seemed not to hear Myron. He was busy scanning the crowd. His eyes fell on the 'sanger family sitting on the platform finishing their biscuits. Climbing the steps quickly, he handed his card to the man, who looked at it and handed it back to him. Littlejim could hear Mr. Bradley as he began to ask questions in a rapid-fire rhythm, which seemed to perplex his listener. Beckoning for the photographer to follow his lead, the writer began to write the man's answers in a leather folder he had opened.

Littlejim and Myron followed to stand and watch. Briskly moving the family to arrange them for the photographer, who was twisting dials and moving about behind the camera, Mr. Bradley continued to talk to the bearded man, now standing beside his wife, who seemed startled to find herself sitting in her husband's presence.

"And, my good fellow," said Mr. Bradley rapidly, pencil poised to write the man's answer, but turning to face the photographer. "Wiley, be sure to get their bare feet into the photo, will you?" Then he turned back to the family. "And how do you make your living?"

"Well," the man said slowly, deliberating the best way to answer this stranger who spoke so quickly. "Well," he repeated. "We do a little 'sanging. And we grow a little corn to get us by when the 'sanging season is over."

Writing quickly on his pad, Mr. Bradley said, "Singing, huh? And what do you sing? The old songs of the hills?"

Myron and Littlejim did not hear the rest of the questions nor the answers. They ran down the platform away from the family, where they exploded into laughter.

"He made the same mistake I made," said Myron, still laughing, removing his glasses to wipe his eyes with his handkerchief.

"I know," said Littlejim, bending double with laughter, "but I was afraid they would think we were making light of them. That would be very unmannerly of us."

"I've stopped laughing," said Myron, sucking in his cheeks, trying to regain control of his laughter as he walked back toward the group. "I want to hear the rest of the interview."

But the photographer was packing up his gear. Mr. Bradley had already closed his writing case and was walking back toward the boys.

"Were they ever crude—and backward? The man was totally illiterate. He did not know what my business card was!" said Mr. Bradley, fairly dancing with delight in rhythm with his speech. "We have a photo of *real hill-billies,* one with their bare feet. That will make a good one to lead the article. I am thinking of using that new word from a film I saw, a word which will liven up the title." Turning to Littlejim, he added, "How do you like being a *'hill-billie'?* Are you a wild, *'hill-billie'* mountaineer, my boy?"

Littlejim was thinking that he did not know what a business card was either. And when he heard *hill-billie,* he immediately did not like it, for the tone of the man's voice made its meaning an unflattering one, no matter what it meant. "Now, Myron," Mr. Bradley went on, not waiting for an answer, "how is your summer down here among the hill-billies?"

"It has been surprising," replied Myron. "I have met some very interesting—"

But Myron was not allowed to finish. "I'll bet *surprising* is too mild a word," said Mr. Bradley, lifting one eyebrow. "I forgot to ask that singing family if they make moonshine whiskey. I wonder if they do. Do you know they were so dumb they could not even give me an answer when I asked them what kind of music they sing. Then when I asked them to sing a few bars for me, they did not seem to understand me either. Is everybody in these mountains that dumb, boy? Are you that dumb, boy?" he asked, turning to Littlejim.

This time Myron interrupted the older man. He spoke loudly, making Littlejim jump in surprise. "*No,* people here are not *dumb*! People here are *not* illiterate! Take Littlejim here. He is the winner of a regional essay competition I wrote you about..."

The train whistle blew.

"Oh, yes," said Mr. Bradley. "Wiley, we need a photograph of this boy." He grabbed Littlejim's arm to pose him in front of a farmer's sled loaded with freight from one of the cars of the train. "Myron says he likes to read. I, for one, doubt that he *can* read! Do you have a book with you, Myron?"

Running to the wagon, Myron brought the book Littlejim had been reading and handed it to him. "Wouldn't Littlejim's essay be more appropriate, Mr. Bradley?" Myron asked.

The train whistle sounded again.

"Hold up the essay, too," said Mr. Bradley, grasping Littlejim's arm and turning him so that the sunlight was directly in his eyes, causing him to flinch. "Take off your cap, young man. You'd look more like a hill-billie if you had overalls, but I guess you'll have to do."

"I've never worn overalls. Only a few men on the Creek wear them," Littlejim tried to explain as he reached up to take off his cap and dropped the book. Picking it up and struggling to unwrap his essay at the same time, he did not realize that he was holding both the book and the newspaper containing his essay upside down. He could hardly see at all. The sun was blinding him. He tried to look at the photographer when a flash of light made him close his eyes in pain.

"That's good, boy," said Mr. Bradley, gathering his pencils and paper to stuff them into his writing case. By the time the red spots had disappeared from Littlejim's eyes, he saw the photographer stepping on the conductor's stool to return to the train.

Mr. Bradley was shaking hands with Myron as he said, "Call me when you get back to civilization. I'll tell your father you look well. I'll send you the article. I got some good local color, thanks to you," he said as he ran for the train. "Good to meet you, too, boy," he called to Littlejim as the train wheels began to roll.

Littlejim and Myron watched in stunned silence as the train passed out of sight around the curve.

"I thought he was coming for a visit," said Littlejim. "Papa and Mama will be disappointed."

"So did I," said Myron, shaking his head. "I had no idea his visit would be so short. Mrs. Zony made arrangements for him to board in Plumtree."

"At least he met a family who 'sangs," said Littlejim.

"But the journalist thought they were so dumb they didn't know what he meant when he asked them what kind of music they sing," Myron replied. The two collapsed with laughter, watched by the family nearby, puzzlement written on their faces, as if they were trying to understand why on earth the young men were laughing.

Chapter 16

"WHERE IS THE MAN from up north?" asked Bigjim, leaning on his mowing scythe as they turned the wagon into the barnyard.

"He had to go on someplace else," Myron quickly explained.

"And you boys wasted a day going into town to get him," said Bigjim, shaking his head in disbelief. "Some folks take no thought of anybody else. You boys"— Littlejim rankled at his father's choice of words—"are to take the team down to Bob's as soon as you curry the horses. I am hiring them out to the lumber company for the next week. Bob will leave tonight as soon as the horses rest awhile. Geneva will have supper done by the time you get back. You are to eat with us, young man, because Zony is away."

"Papa, you aren't hiring out the team for some other man to handle?" said Littlejim in despair. "What if he doesn't take care of them!"

"Bob's as good a man with a team as any in the county," said Bigjim sadly. "I would go too if they needed a man, but he says they have more men than they need. I have to get hold of some cash money, any way I can."

Littlejim knew that hiring the team out for another man to work, even Uncle Bob, meant that his father was desperate. He could not imagine his father agreeing to do such a thing. He had started to protest, but one look at his papa's face stopped his words. Until that moment Littlejim had not noticed how different Bigjim looked since Mama's illness, with his usually square shoulders stooped, his face gray, and his eyes red-rimmed under the old slouch hat he wore for working around the farm and in the woods. Littlejim and Myron watched Bigjim walk away, his shoulders sagging, his step slower than his son could ever remember.

As the boys walked back from the barn, they heard voices and watched as Bigjim offered his arm to help the Dr. Mrs. Sloop down the steep path to the road. Stopping to wave, Littlejim opened his mouth to call a greeting but was stopped by the doctor's words.

"She needs treatment we cannot provide," said Dr. Mrs. Sloop, her face mirroring the worry in the tall man's face as she looked up at him. "We have very little medicine that will help. She needs to be in a hospital. Have you told her yet?"

Littlejim saw his father wipe his eyes on his sleeve,

with grass and dust clinging to its fabric from the mowing, and he heard his papa say, in a choked voice, "I
don't know what to do, Dr. Sloop. The timber business
has all but dried up here on the Creek since the war is
over. I can't seem to get my hands on any cash money
to take her to the hospital."

"Jim, please allow me to write to my friends in
Statesville. Perhaps they can help." The lady patted
Bigjim's arm, comforting an old friend. She and Dr. Mr.
Sloop had cared for his family since opening the office
in Plumtree.

"We don't take charity. You know that, ma'am.
You've been acquainted with us a long time," said Bigjim
emphatically.

"This will not be charity, my old friend," said the
doctor. "I'm sure they would think some of your good
hams ample repayment for their help. Good hams would
be worth more than dollars to them."

"That would make their help easier to take, I
reckon," said Bigjim. "And I am much obliged."

Littlejim felt all the wind leave his lungs. He had
thought his mother was growing stronger. He had no
idea the sickness was serious enough for her to go to a
hospital. Turning to walk ahead of Myron, he tried to
hide the tears that stung his eyes.

A hand gripped his shoulder firmly. "I had no idea
your mother was so ill," said Myron. "Perhaps my family
could help."

"Papa would never take charity," said Littlejim. "And he doesn't borrow. We take care of our own." Hearing his own voice saying such words, he sounded just like his father, a realization that shocked him. But now he realized why his father was willing to hire out the team, the horses that were his pride and joy. That realization only made Littlejim more determined to find a way to help his mama. Oh, how he wanted to go away to school, to learn to fly an aeroplane, to do all of the things he had dreamed of, but he would have time to do those things later. Right now, his family had to come first, and that was that.

"We'll find a way," said Myron. "Your mother needs medical treatment. We *must* find a way."

Chapter 17

YOU BOYS WANT some of Geneva's corn bread? Zony left word that you were to take supper with us while she is away at the college in Boone." Bigjim's voice came to his son's ears gruffly as he joined the young men on the path. Pulling his hat down so that they could not see his eyes, he pushed past them and climbed to the porch, poured some water from the bucket there, and washed his face and hands, drying them on the homespun towel hanging beside the mirror.

Littlejim and Myron watched frozen in silence, trying by unspoken agreement not to intrude on the pain written on his face as he combed his hair and dusted the grass from his clothing.

"I am truly sorry," said Myron quietly. "I am so sorry."

Littlejim nodded his head as they entered the kitchen, afraid that if he spoke, his friend would know he was about to cry.

As the family gathered around the table, for the first time in Littlejim's memory they did not wait for Bigjim to ask the blessing and prepare to eat.

As Aunt Geneva said, "Let us bow our heads and grace the table," Myron looked at Littlejim for guidance.

Littlejim reached out to take his friend's large hand, now callused from farmwork, with his right hand and May's tiny soft one with his left as they formed a circle to say together,

"Come, dear Lord and be our guest.
Let this food to us be blest. Amen."

The lump in Littlejim's throat grew larger as May squeezed his hand. He was remembering a time, when he was not much older than she, when Mama had taught him to say the blessing in German with her. He liked it more in the foreign language. Perhaps that was because he and Mama only said it in German when Bigjim was away. That was a special thing they shared.

Aunt Geneva asked, "Would you like some fresh tomatoes with your beans, Jimmy?"

"Yes, ma'am," he said in a whisper. The first tomatoes from the garden were always a treat. But today he was not hungry, although his stomach felt hollow and empty.

He had taken his first bite when voices sounded in the front yard.

"Go see what is going on, please, Jimmy?" said Aunt

Geneva. "I don't want visitors to disturb your mother."

"May I please be excused to go with him?" asked Myron.

As they made their way around the porch from the kitchen, Bigjim came out the front door, carefully closing it behind him. At the steps a stranger leaned on a cane with a gold head. He looked familiar, but Littlejim could not place his face. At the stranger's side stood Dearborne Guinn, one of the sawyers from Uncle Bob's mill, a man who was never one of Littlejim's favorites. He stood nervously turning his hat around and around in his hands.

"Jim, this is Philmore Thorn. He is with the Triangle Mineral and Mining Company out of Baltimore," said Mr. Guinn. "He would like to talk some business with you, if you've the time."

Littlejim was furious. Mr. Guinn had no business speaking like that to a man of his father's standing in the community when, as far as the boy knew, he barely knew Bigjim. Guinn had grown up on the River Road, so he knew it was the mountain way to address any adult outside one's own family with a formal title, usually Mr. or Mrs. and their family name.

"State your business, Mr. Thorn," said Bigjim, not moving to shake the man's hand, to Littlejim's surprise, but drawing himself up to stand stiffly at the top of his steps. "I've yet to eat my supper. And my wife is poorly."

Littlejim thought his papa's manner unseemly until

he realized that Bigjim's behavior meant he was keeping his distance until he learned Mr. Guinn's reasons for calling at mealtime at the door of people with whom he was barely acquainted.

Mr. Thorn placed one booted foot on the bottom step as if to minimize the distance between them and to stake his claim to greater territory. Littlejim felt revulsion and anger draw his hands into fists as they hung by his side.

"Mr. Houston," said Mr. Thorn in a condescending manner, "I am here representing a group of very knowledgeable men up in the industrialized northern part of our nation. These men have reason to believe that this area may be rich in valuable minerals. I have been authorized to scout this area for good prospects for mining such minerals and to offer a good price for the purchase of mineral rights."

"Mineral rights?" repeated Bigjim. "Explain yourself."

"It's a good proposition for the landowner such as yourself, my good man. We take all the risks. You sell us the rights to prospect for minerals under your property, if we find nothing, you remain the landowner. If we find something of value, you share in the profits. In the end, you still own the land, whatever happens. That's a fair proposition, don't you agree?" The man smiled warmly but, Littlejim thought, insincerely up at Bigjim, whose fists were also clenched at his sides, visible to his son and to Myron but not to the visitors in the yard.

"How much an acre?" asked Bigjim, trying not to sound eager. His son knew he prided himself on being a good horse trader, one who never allowed the other person to know that he wanted to buy or sell, pretending the sale did not matter to him at all.

"How many acres you got here?" asked Mr. Thorn.

"About a hundred, give or take a few, I would reckon," said Mr. Guinn.

"Thereabouts," agreed Bigjim. "How much prospecting do you intend to do?" He stopped, as if considering a remote possibility. "*If* I decide to sell you these rights?"

"Only what is necessary to locate the minerals your soil may be hiding," assured Mr. Thorn.

"What do you say, Jim?" asked Mr. Guinn. "This is a *good* deal."

"What is your interest in all this, Dearborne?" asked Bigjim. "I thought you left with Bob to work in the big timber operations."

"Just being neighborly," the man answered with a nervous laugh, his words falling over one another. "I thought my neighbors deserved some of the good fortune befalling us here. The big companies are going to offer us a better life in a new time. Things have changed a lot up north since the Great War. Cities. Factories. Big money. Things will be a-changing here too. Yes sir, good times a-coming to these hills now that the old ways are dying out. I want my neighbors to be part of that good fortune a-coming with the changing times. What do you say, Jim?" In his excitement Dearborne seemed to gasp for air as he finished his speech.

Littlejim watched his father consider what the man said for a few moments, which seemed to be an eternity, then finally answer, "I'll talk to you about it tomorrow evening. Give me some time to consider it."

"You won't back out now, will you, my good man?" asked Mr. Thorn. "This offer won't last forever. If your neighbors sell us all the rights we need, you'll be left out in the cold."

Littlejim saw his father hesitate for a second before replying, "A man's word is as good as his bond. I will give you an answer about this time tomorrow."

"If everybody else on the Creek sells to us before that time, we won't need to see you," said Mr. Guinn. "We've already talked to every other man on the Creek."

Littlejim suddenly remembered Mr. Greene's warning in the hotel that day. He had forgotten to give his father the message. "Papa," said Littlejim quietly. "Mr. Greene said we should be suspicious of mineral speculators."

As the two men glanced at each other, then frowned at Littlejim, his father said again, "A man's word is his bond. I expect you to be here about this time tomorrow." And Bigjim walked through the door.

Littlejim watched the two men climb down the hill path to their carriage.

"That man was on the train I came here on," said Myron. "I don't trust him."

"That's where I've seen him," said Littlejim. "Mr. Greene told me to warn Papa, but I forgot to tell him. What do you think Papa should do?"

"I don't know," said Myron. "This is the first time I've wished my father could be here. He is a good attorney. He would know what to do."

"This might be a way to get Mama to the hospital," said Littlejim.

"You're right," agreed Myron. "Perhaps the sale will provide the means. We must find a way."

Chapter 18

BIGJIM SAT ON THE front porch in the twilight, far from Mama's window, talking with his young guest. Littlejim joined them when the chores were finished.

"Let me telegraph my father for his opinion before you sign anything," suggested Myron. "We can send him a copy of the agreement Mr. Thorn offers, and he will know what to do."

"The nearest telegraph is in Spruce Pine or in Cranberry; either is a day's journey from here. If I only had a good saddle horse, one which could stand up to running hard all day. But every horse and ox on the Creek has been hired out to the lumber companies. I just don't know what to do."

"Do you think we could borrow a saddle horse from Mr. Burleson, Papa? Or perhaps he would drive us in his auty-mobile," said Littlejim. "I could work for him in exchange. Please, Papa."

"All of his horses and his auty-mobile are rented out

to the summer people who went on a pack trip to Roan Mountain. I saw them pass here today. Even Zony's gone this week in her buggy to a teacher's meeting at the college. I don't think an animal except a few cows are to be found, and most of them have been sent to the high pastures," said Bigjim. "I guess we will have to take Dearborne as a man of his word. Never heard of him being dishonest. Likes to make a dollar without putting forth much effort is the worst I've heard about him."

But Littlejim had a fearful knot in his stomach. "I don't know if we should trust him."

"Son, if a man can't have faith in his neighbors," said Bigjim, "then I don't know what this world is coming to, do you?"

Littlejim chewed on his lower lip, trying not to interfere. An argument would only make his father more resolved than ever that his decision to trust Mr. Guinn was the right one.

"You know, Mr. Houston," said Myron, "these mountains are so beautiful and the way of life is so pleasant, this is a good place to live except for the problem of transportation. The roads here are terrible. No place should be so isolated that it takes a day to reach a telegraph station or a train!"

"Roads in these hills are not high on the list of the legislature's priorities," said Bigjim, laughing scornfully. "Most elections in the mountain counties go the wrong way. The mountain counties vote Republican in a Democrat state. Legislators are not likely to spend money on roads for a few people who probably voted *again'* them when they can spend money on a lot of people who can, and probably did, vote *for* them."

"It isn't fair!" said Myron. "This is a democracy. We are supposed to be created equal. The people here are not treated as equals. That isn't fair!"

Bigjim got up from his chair and said sadly, "It ain't fair that I work hard to support my family, and yet I cannot afford to get the doctoring my good wife needs. Selling the mineral rights seems to be the only answer, what with timber prices under the floor and all. That doesn't seem fair either."

"Mr. Greene said he wanted to help," Littlejim said. "He said he would be up to talk to you. He said you should be careful."

"A man who's any kind of a man has to make up his own mind," said his father. "He don't talk of his family's affairs with outsiders either."

"But Papa," said Littlejim, trying to will his father to get help in making the decision. "Mr. Greene said he wanted to talk with you. He said we should be careful."

His father sat in silence, his shoulders drooping, then said, "Anyway, George Greene is a half day's ride from here, even if I had a good horse," said Bigjim. "I wish he had told you just how I should be careful. It's a sad time when a man can't trust his neighbors."

Chapter 19

ALL THE FOLLOWING DAY as they worked in the cornfield, Littlejim and Myron discussed the problems the family faced. When they met Bigjim at the washbasin at supper time, they had all come to the same conclusion.

"Hold out for at least one dollar an acre," urged Myron as they watched the mineral speculators climb the hill after supper.

"Well, Jim," said Mr. Guinn. "I certainly hope you have come to your senses and see the opportunities open to you here."

"Didn't know I had lost any of my senses, Dearborne," said Bigjim sarcastically. "At least, none that you'd know of."

Myron and Littlejim looked at each other as if to say, "He can take care of himself."

"Now," said Mr. Thorn placatingly, "I'm sure, being the man of good sense that he is, Mr. Houston will make a good decision, whatever he decides. Of course in my opinion, you could only make one decision in this case."

"How much you offering per acre?" asked Bigjim abruptly to end the nonsense.

"Well, it will cost the company a lot of money to do the prospecting," said Mr. Thorn. "I think fifty cents an acre is a fair price."

"And what percentage of any mineral profits will go to Mr. Houston?" asked Myron in his most formal manner.

"And just who is this *boy*?" asked Mr. Guinn.

Ignoring the insult, Myron stood up and bowed slightly. "I am his attorney, Myron Farber of Philadelphia. I am here to advise Mr. Houston not to accept one penny under one dollar per acre. Now what is his percentage of profits?"

Bigjim's eyes widened as he opened his mouth to speak, but then closed it quickly, and said nothing.

Mr. Guinn and Mr. Thorn looked at each other. Mr. Thorn shrugged his shoulders. "I think five percent should be a fair percentage," he said. "That's standard," he added quickly.

"Could we see the contract, please?" asked Myron. "We need to read it carefully before Mr. Houston signs anything."

Opening the valise at his side, Mr. Guinn pulled out a stack of papers and began to sort through them. Finally he found the contract.

"Of course, we will have to make a few changes," he said, with a knowing look at Mr. Thorn. Pulling out his pen and ink, he began to change words and numbers.

Myron walked over to look over his shoulder. Mr. Guinn moved away so that Myron could not see the paper. Myron moved again so that he could read over the man's shoulder. Guinn drew the paper closer to his chest to hide its contents. When he had finished writing, he handed the document to Mr. Thorn, who read it and handed it to Myron, who read it aloud, explaining what the legal terms meant as he read.

"Exactly how is the term *prospect* defined here?" asked Myron.

"It means that the company has the right to make tunnels and borings or to take any actions necessary to prepare the land for prospecting the minerals. In other words, to take whatever steps are necessary to gain access to the minerals located on this land," Mr. Thorn hurried to explain.

Mr. Guinn smiled and added, "And when we are finished, the land belongs to Mr. Houston, just as it always did."

"So you will pay Mr. Houston one dollar per acre for one hundred acres, more or less," restated Myron. "Then you will pay him five percent of the profits from the sale of minerals you find on or under his land. After you have finished, the land belongs solely to Mr. Houston. Am I correct?"

"You have got yourself one good lawyer, Mr. Houston," said Mr. Guinn. "He drives a hard bargain."

Bigjim read the document slowly, forming the words with his lips, then took the pen. Slowly and laboriously, he signed his name where Mr. Thorn had pointed on the page.

"Would you boys witness this?" asked Mr. Thorn, handing the paper first to Myron.

When the papers were signed, Mr. Thorn took out a book of banknotes, wrote on the note, and offered it. Myron put out his hand between the note and Bigjim. "Cash," he said. "Mr. Houston only deals in hard cash. Otherwise the deal is off."

The two men looked at each other once more.

"But Mr. Farber—is that your name? Our company only deals in banknotes. Good at any bank. All Mr. Houston has to do is ask for cash at the bank," said Mr. Thorn placatingly.

"The bank is a day's journey from here," said Myron patiently. "Mr. Houston's work keeps him far too busy to travel to a bank." Stepping between Bigjim and the men, Myron folded his arms and said sternly, "Cash, please, if you wish to do business with Mr. Houston."

The two men looked at each other again. Finally Mr. Thorn took a large wallet from his coat pocket and, as Myron stepped out of the way, counted the green bills into Bigjim's hands.

"We would also like a copy of the contract for Mr.

Houston's records," added Myron, stepping back into the center of the group.

When he had copied all the changes and each man had signed his name again, Myron checked the contract and handed the second copy to Bigjim.

"Pleasure doing business with you, gentlemen," said Mr. Thorn, shaking hands with Bigjim, and then with Myron.

Then, taking over the situation, Myron led the men away from the house, saying, "And now, gentlemen, Mr. Houston's wife is very ill. He needs to spend the rest of the evening with her." He guided them down the path to the road.

Littlejim sat stunned. He had never seen anyone control his father's behavior as Myron had done.

As the men drove out of sight, Myron said, "I am worried about their interpretation of the word *prospect*. It *is* open to interpretation."

But Bigjim was almost in shock. "You got me one hundred dollars cash money," he told Myron. "I can hardly believe it."

"We had no way of knowing if their banknote is good or not," said Myron. "U.S. currency is usually good anywhere."

"One hundred dollars cash money," repeated Bigjim.

"You will need to get a real attorney to read that contract when you get into town," said Myron. "Or we can wire it to my father."

"Now I can take Gertrude to the hospital," said

Bigjim, shaking his head in disbelief and reaching out to shake hands, but lowering his head so that the younger man could not see his eyes. "Young man, I am indeed much obliged to you this day."

Littlejim offered his hand as well. "Much obliged," he said, but Mr. Greene's words echoed in his ears.

"I only hope that I read that contract accurately," said Myron.

Chapter 20

THE FOLLOWING WEEK Mr. Vance loaned his automobile and driver, now returned by the summer visitors, to carry Mama and Bigjim down the mountain to the hospital in Statesville. The automobile waited in the side yard, with a basket of food and a crock of cool water for their journey.

Littlejim felt his heart sink as he saw how small and frail his mother looked as Bigjim carried her down the steps. Watching it chug out into the meadow and down into the road, the family gathered on top of the embankment to wave. Littlejim's throat ached when Mama weakly waved back at them. Looking down at Nell, he realized she was crying. Even May's little songs had stopped. She sat on the steps, her chin resting on her fists, alone and dejected.

Throwing one arm awkwardly around her shoulders, he said, "Don't cry. Mama is going to the hospital so the doctors there can make her well."

"Do you think she will ever come back?" asked Nell. "I've never known anybody who went to a hospital."

"Of course. Mama won't leave us. She loves us," he said. He spoke with a reassurance he did not feel. That Mama might not return was his greatest fear, which he dared not voice.

"I miss Mama already," said Nell. "What can we do?"

"I know," said Littlejim, frantically searching for something that would help turn their minds from the sorrow of Mama's going away to the hospital. He stood frozen, then he had an idea.

"Let's go to the woodshed and make some flutter mills. Mama always likes to see them blowing in the wind. When she returns, maybe we'll fill the yard with flutter mills, and when she comes around the bend, they will all be turning in the front yard. She would like that, don't you think?"

Nell smiled. "Oh, Littlejim. That's a good idea. Let's start now and we'll be ready when she comes home."

Swooping May up from the grass where she was examining a bumblebee far too carefully for her own good, Littlejim sat her on his shoulders as she crowed with delight and pulled his hair. Nell skipped along beside them. Littlejim was glad to see her mood change to one of hope.

Unlocking the woodshed, he placed May in a small pen where Mama kept baby chicks, or baby *dibs*, as Nell called them, each spring, its wire walls forming a safety net that would protect his little sister. Placing a stack of odd blocks of wood in the center of the pen, he took a small block and hit the stack as if driving a nail. May picked up another block and began to beat on the stack, calling to her brother to see if he was watching her accomplishments.

"You can build all day," he said. "Safely. We can't have you getting hurt. Nell, you can use my small tools. They will just fit your hands."

For more than a year he had possessed a key to his father's tool case, but he still preferred to use the tools St. Nicholas had brought him. Each time he used a small hammer or saw, he could recall the wonder of that Christmas a few years ago when Mama had spent her butter and egg money to make his Christmas dream come true. He could recall the joy of that night and the taste of peppermint, as his heart was filled with gratitude as he thought of Mama's love for him. But now his heart was saddened that she was so ill, and he was filled with despair that she might not return to be with their family.

Nell had gathered the scraps of wood they would use for the fluttermills and carried them to the workbench, where Littlejim selected appropriate pieces for each of the parts of the fluttermills and arranged them in stacks. As she polished the small wind blades they had created on a rainy day in early summer, he gouged a tiny hole to attach the blades to the body of the fluttermill.

As May beat happily, singing her little song with words no one could understand, and Nell worked diligently, Littlejim found that the noise and activity began to lighten his heart. Nell was busy mixing some of Mama's dyes to paint the blades of the fluttermills when Myron opened the door to find Littlejim whistling a tune under his breath.

"I have a surprise," he said, stopping to pick up one of the blades. "What are these things?"

Nell handed him a completed mill. "Aren't they pretty? Littlejim builds them. Some are run by the wind, and some of them go in the creek for the water to turn them."

"They are wonderful," said Myron. "I think you could sell these to a toy store in Philadelphia. May I have one?"

"You mean there are stores just for toys?" asked Nell in amazement.

"Yes, Miss Nell, entire stores filled with toys and dolls of every description!" said Myron expansively. "You will have to come to Philadelphia to visit. We'll visit such a store," he teased.

"When?" asked Nell, ready to leave immediately.

"When you grow up," said Myron. "Littlejim, I have a surprise for you."

"When I grow up, I won't be interested in going to a toy store," insisted Nell. "I want to go now."

"You have started something," said Littlejim in a whisper to Myron. "She will never stop asking until she gets to Philadelphia."

Chapter 21

ALTHOUGH THE FAMILY missed Mama and Bigjim, the summer was passing quickly. Soon July Fourth came, but the family did not go to the Bald to celebrate with the community. It was too far to walk and carry the food, Aunt Geneva said. Scott and Swain were still hired out to Uncle Bob so the money could be sent to Papa and Mama down in Statesville. Tarp was away with his wagon and horses.

Aunt Zony and her family decided not to attend the community July Fourth celebration, either, and invited Aunt Geneva, Littlejim, Nell, and May to join them at noonday dinner on the ground in the meadow near the creek. Myron and Littlejim carried the cane poles with them so they could fish after the meal. They spent the afternoon sitting in the cool shade of the willows and caught enough fish for a fish supper that night. Although Littlejim remembered the excitement of the last two Fourth of July's, he thought that this quiet day was one he would always remember, not only because it had been a pleasant celebration, but because he missed having his parents as part of the celebration this year.

The following week they joined most of the community at the homecoming at the church with its all-day singing and dinner-on-the-ground. This was a new experience for Myron. After the singing, he and Littlejim tried to eat something from the dinner brought by every family in attendance. That afternoon, too, they found their way back to the bank of the Creek, where they pulled off their shoes and stockings to cool their feet in the rushing water and lay quietly trying to calm their aching stomachs, stuffed with far too much good food.

Chores on the farm kept the family busy. The vegetable garden had to be tended, vegetables gathered, washed, canned, dried, and preserved for the winter. Summer apples were picked and stored in the root cellar. Cherries ripened and were pitted and dried for winter pies. Corn had to be carried to the mill downriver to be ground into cornmeal. Blackberries ripened and filled all the pails in the house, to be boiled with sugar into jam. And letters were written to Bigjim and Mama at least twice a week so they were assured that food was being preserved for winter, and were kept abreast of the happenings up and down the Creek. So far, though, there had been no word back from Papa. Aunt Geneva said no news is good news, and Littlejim wanted to believe that.

One rainy day in late July Littlejim and Nell were

working on the fluttermills when Myron opened the door.

"*Harper's Monthly* came today," said Myron as he sat on the bench beside Littlejim. "I waited to open it until I came up here. Your photograph should be in it."

Ripping off the brown cover, he checked the table of contents and turned to the article, " 'Visiting the Hills—and the Hill-billies,' " he read. "Ouch," he said, pushing his glasses up on his nose to hide his embarrassment at the discomfort he could see on Littlejim's face. "That must be the new word for people who don't live in the city. I don't think I like the sound of it."

"I don't either," said Littlejim, not looking up. "Read the article to me."

"No, look. Here is your photograph," Myron said, thrusting the magazine under Littlejim's face as Nell moved closer for a better view.

Myron read the caption aloud, " 'Country came to town. An illiterate mountain boy from the backwoods has come to town to watch the train come in, a big Saturday treat, in the tiny mountain town of Spruce Pine, North Carolina. This hill-billie claims to be reading the book, but you will notice that he holds it and the newspaper upside down.' "

Looking back from the magazine was a horrible photograph of himself, squinting into the sun, his expression that of a startled animal, holding the book he had been reading with the title upside down.

"That's awful," said Nell. "That picture makes you look dumb."

Myron was silent. Littlejim got up and walked outside, closing the door behind him, slamming it hard. He hated that travel writer, he thought. He hated the photographer. And he hated Myron. He wished the summer would end so that he would go back to Philadelphia, where he belonged. Littlejim's anger had to go somewhere, so he turned around and hit the door with his fist, scraping his knuckles. He threw his back against the wall, licked his knuckles, and tried not to let his tears of anger leave his eyes.

Myron opened the door uneasily. "I'm sorry," he said. "I had no idea he would be so callous and so dishonest."

"You're sorry?!" shouted Littlejim. "It is not a picture of you there, being branded as illiterate. You just want to ridicule us. That's why you brought him here! I wish I had never seen you or him."

"Littlejim," said Myron. "I have come to think of you as my good friend. I would never do something like this to a friend. It is my responsibility for bringing him, but I have grown to like and respect the people here. I would never do something to make you or anyone else here feel bad. I apologize."

Nell stuck her head out the door. "What does *illiterate* mean?" she asked. "It says here you are illiterate."

"It means 'a person who cannot read,' " snapped Littlejim.

"You can read!" protested Nell. "You are the best student in Mr. Osk's school. You read all the time."

"And you won a writing competition in a major newspaper from a large city. You are in a national competition now," said Myron quietly as beads of sweat formed on his upper lip. "I am sorry Mr. Bradley is so ignorant and hateful. I will write him."

"Why would he tell a lie like that?" asked Littlejim, walking back into the shed to place his tools back in their case.

"I don't know," said Myron, shaking his head. "I have read his articles. I always assumed they were accurate. I knew him through my father's firm. A lot of writers have written that mountain people are ignorant and illiterate. That's what I thought. Remember how I behaved toward you and Nell?"

"I remember!" said Nell, with a look of scorn in Myron's direction.

"All of the photography I have seen of Appalachian mountaineers has shown people who looked backward. It never occurred to me the photographs might be inaccurate. But this one is," Myron said, his face drawn with the pain of having caused humiliation.

Littlejim said nothing, rearranging his tools, keeping his eyes focused on his activities so that Myron would not guess how big the lump in his throat had grown.

"Perhaps Mr. Bradley only heard and saw what he came here expecting. He did not listen when I told him about you," Myron continued. "My father says that when we travel to other countries, we look at people through our expectations. Evidence which does not fit our expectations is ignored. Mr. Bradley certainly was not around long enough to have his expectations changed!"

"You don't have to defend your friend," said Little-jim in a hard whisper.

"I wasn't defending him," said Myron. "I am angry that you have been humiliated. I am only trying to understand the ignorance of a man who ridicules and disparages others based on his assumptions. It's as if he does not realize that people who are different from him are human and have feelings. I am *so* sorry."

Ignoring the two boys, Nell had taken the magazine and was reading. "What does this mean? It says 'I asked the head of this barefoot hill-billie family what he did for a living, and he answered, "We sang." But when I asked, "What kind of music do you sing?" the man did not understand what I meant. How can such ignorance exist in this modern age?' "

Looking up at the pair standing beside the bench, Nell said, "Everybody knows the man meant his family digs ginseng from the places it grows in the woods, not that they sing." And she sang a few notes, "La, la, la." She stopped to think, then said adamantly, "That writer is pretty ignorant, if you ask me."

Littlejim and Myron looked at each other for a moment and then burst out laughing. The tension was broken. Littlejim felt his hurt and anger melting as he watched Myron, imaginary pen and pad in hand, his nose in the air with his glasses balanced on the tip, mimicking Bennington Bradley.

"And what do you do for a living, my good man?" asked Myron, walking back and forth hurriedly in small prancing steps while pretending to write.

Littlejim answered in a quavering voice, stopping to emphasize each word, "Well. Sir. My poor. Ignorant. Barefoot. Backwoods family. We 'sang. Sir."

Myron pranced forward and bowed, "And what kind of music do you 'sang, my good man?"

"We 'sang ginseng, sir, ginseng wherever it grows," sang Littlejim. "La, la, la." Together they sang the words again. And again. And again.

Nell watched in disgust as they fell on the floor, rolling in the sawdust and shavings, screaming with laughter as May joined the merriment, singing "La, la, la."

Finally Myron sat up and brushed himself off, pulling the shavings from his pants and shirt.

"I am relieved that you can laugh at ignorance when the man printed lies about you and embarrassed you," said Myron. "I doubt if I could."

"It hurts," said Littlejim, pushing shavings out of his hair. "It hurts to have all the readers of the magazine think I am illiterate and ignorant."

"How do you think that poor family of 'sangers will feel when they read this?" asked Nell.

"I don't think they will see it," said Littlejim. "I doubt that they have magazines available."

"That does not forgive him for writing so cruelly about those people," said Myron. "Now people all over the nation will have evidence that mountain people are as poor, ignorant, and backward as Mr. Bradley has portrayed them. I'll bet we have people just like them in Philadelphia, but he would never be so cruel about them. That might reflect on our *city of brotherly love*. Ha."

"I am going to write him a letter, too," said Littlejim, growing silent as he realized that standing up for himself to an outsider would have seemed to him unmannerly only a short time ago. He had watched Myron stand up to the mineral speculators. Now he realized that defending himself was more important than trying not to hurt a cruel man's feelings. "I have learned a lot from you," he added after a while.

"And I have learned from you, too, my friend," said Myron. "This summer has changed each of us, I guess."

"I think we need to tell him that telling lies about others is wrong," said Nell as the three friends sat around the kitchen table the next night, the kerosene lamp shedding light on their sheets of paper.

"He won't understand that he told a lie," said Myron. "He thinks he wrote what he saw here."

"But you must tell him the truth," Nell insisted, pointing to the piece of paper on which Myron was writing furiously.

"Here is my letter," said Myron finally. "Let me read it to you:

"Dear Mr. Bradley,

"Your short stop recently at the train station in Spruce Pine, hasty in the extreme, did the people and the place a grave injustice when your article appeared in the latest issue of the magazine. You have given the impression that everyone here is illiterate, backward, and poor. You published a horrible photograph of my friend, Littlejim Houston, and you called him illiterate. In fact, this young man won a regional competition for a fine essay, and he is now competing nationally for a scholarship. He is the best student at his small local school. I have spent the summer with his family, and I know he has a fine mind; he is well-read and would be considered well educated for his age. His family reads books, newspapers, and magazines. They are as knowledgeable about current affairs as many of my university friends. To portray them otherwise, as you did in the article, is unfair and dishonest in the extreme.

"When I wrote to you suggesting that you visit, I hoped you would get to know the family I am visiting and learn about the people here in the mountains. Yes, their lives are different from the cities where we live. Some of the modern inventions common in Philadelphia are not yet part of this community. However, if you had taken the time to get to know them, you would find people who are fair, courteous, intelligent, and *literate* here.

"Therefore, I am writing this letter to ask that you, as a business associate of my father, please publish my letter so your readers will have the facts about my friend. I am enclosing a copy of my friend's award-winning essay. I hope you will read it this time and will realize that you were wrong in judging him and his people.

"With best regards,

"Myron Farber"

"That's a very good letter," said Nell.

Half listening, Littlejim sat across the table concentrating on the letter he was writing, but stopped to nod his approval when Myron had finished.

"You've said everything," he finally said to Myron. "I don't know what else to say."

"If we want to prove you are literate, you must write a letter," said Myron. "Why don't you write how cruel he was to the poor family of 'sangers?"

As he said the words, Myron and Littlejim looked at one another and exploded with laughter as they said in unison, "What kind of music do you *sang,* my good man?"

Nell shook her head in disgust. She had heard that play on words before, and she was tired of it.

When the boys had finally settled down again, Nell brought out a plate of walnut cookies and offered one to Myron.

"*Warnet* cookies," said Littlejim, grinning. Papa calls them *warnet* cookies. He mispronounces it every time. Maybe he should *sang,* too." But as he said the words, he felt guilt for ridiculing his papa, and for a moment he missed his parents deeply.

"Are you sure?" asked Myron, helping himself to another cookie. "I had a Shakespeare class at college. My professor told us that many words were pronounced differently in those days. In one of the plays, I've forgotten which one, he had *quiver* rhyme with *cover.* The professor told us that Shakespeare would have said *kiver.* I've always found that strange."

"Papa says 'the kivers on the bed,' " offered Nell.

"He does," agreed Littlejim, biting into a cookie.

"A great many things from the past are still alive here," said Myron. "Perhaps the language is, too. When did your family come to this valley?"

"Papa says we, or our first grandsire, came here in 1762," said Littlejim. "Got a land grant from the king of England."

"You know a great many things, really," said Myron.

"I don't have any idea when my ancestors arrived here. I think it was my grandfather, though."

"I guess most people here know about the past times in their families," said Littlejim. "I remember Preacher Hall saying that the past is an important part of now. *Now* would you like to hear my letter?

"Dear Mr. Bradley,

"I am writing this letter to show you that I am not illiterate and that I am not ignorant. I am the best pupil in Mr. Osk's school. My parents have also taught me that to call a person ignorant, especially if that person has had fewer opportunities than I have, is unmannerly.

"My aunt Zony says that we are all ignorant, but that we are all ignorant about different things. For instance, you are ignorant of some things that the poor man in your other photograph knows. He knew that *to sang* means *to dig ginseng.* You did not. You assumed that he was mispronouncing *to sing.* I am sure that the man also knows a great deal about plants and the woods hereabouts, knowledge which you have not learned in the city. I am also sure that you know a great many things he does not, but to behave toward others in an unmannerly and thoughtless way shows a great deal of ignorance.

"I am also writing to tell you that your photograph of me made me feel very bad. The sun was in my eyes, and when I picked up the book I was reading I could not see that it was upside down. Your photograph of me made me look dumb, and you wrote that I am illiterate. Neither of those things is true. Here is a photograph of me from the *Kansas City Star,* so you can see what I look like and a copy of my essay to prove I am not illiterate.

"When you come back to the Blue Ridge Mountains again, I hope you will stay long enough to learn the truth about us, so you will not make fun of us.

"With best regards,

"Jimmy Houston"

"I am glad you said he was ignorant, too," said Myron.

"I hope I wasn't too unmannerly," said Littlejim. "I guess he could get his feelings hurt by what I say, too."

"I hope so," said Myron. "He deserves it."

"Mama says we should always consider the other person's feelings as well as our own," said Littlejim, suddenly missing Mama more than he had at any other time since she went away to the hospital.

"Aunt Geneva got a letter from Mama yesterday. She wrote that the doctors had operated on her and she was feeling stronger every day. She asked Aunt Geneva to make us these cookies," said Nell. "So we would remember that she still loves us."

"I miss her," said Littlejim, feeling bad that, in his embarrassment over the article and the photograph, he had forgotten how sick Mama was and how he wished she would come home soon. Then he realized that he missed Papa, too. It had seemed like such a long time since she and Bigjim had left for the hospital. Every day Littlejim had thought of them and wished for a letter to come. With all that was going on, he had forgotten about them on the very day the letter arrived. At first he felt guilty about forgetting, then his feelings turned to joy that she was well enough to write to them the letter they had waited so long to receive.

"Mama wrote that finally she was able to sit in her chair and write to let us know that we are in her thoughts and prayers every day," Nell said.

"Let's write her a letter back," said Littlejim. "We will send her all sorts of good wishes to help make her well."

Chapter 22

FINALLY, ONE DAY in late summer, Uncle Bob brought the horses back to the farm. "They have been well fed," he said. "But they could use a few days of summer pasture."

Littlejim thought that would be a good idea, but the horses were needed first to take Myron to the train station for his trip home to Philadelphia. Then they could be put out to pasture.

"The summer has passed awfully fast," said Littlejim as the boys loaded Myron's trunk into the wagon. Scott and Swain stamped their big feet, indicating that they were eager to begin their journey. "With Mama and Papa away, I don't know what we would have done without your help." He was wanting to find a way, without embarrassing himself, to tell Myron that he would miss him.

"Yes, the summer has passed very fast," agreed Myron. "I thought I would miss the city, but I have had a good time. I shall miss the smell of drying hay and of Aunt Geneva's kitchen fire"—he sniffed the air around him—"and the taste of biscuits and corn bread and fresh vegetables. I will miss your family, too." He kicked the toe of his boot into the dust, trying to hide his embarrassment and looking for a way to tell Littlejim how much he would miss him.

"I'll miss…" Littlejim and Myron spoke at the same time as Nell came bounding down the steps, saying, "And I will miss you until I can finish Mr. Osk's school, so I can come to Philadelphia, too. Will you miss me, too?"

"Yes, Nell," said Myron, laughing and giving her a brotherly hug. "Until you finish Mr. Osk's school and come to visit us. But I hope to come back here before that time."

"I'm going to study hard," she assured him. "I'm going to pick up the mail," she sang happily. "I saw Wil Hullinder at Aunt Zony's mailbox. Maybe we have a letter from Mama and Papa. I hope so."

"I hope your mother is recovering from her surgery and will soon be well," said Myron. "Remember, my father could loan you money if you need it."

"We'll be all right. As you know, we grow most of what we eat," said Littlejim. "We make most of what we need. The only reason we have need for hard cash is for Mama's doctors and medicine. Papa's earnings from timbering have given us a pretty good living—until the timbering dried up."

"I hope you win the scholarship, too," said Myron. "But if you don't, my family will help you, I know."

"Mama and Papa don't believe in borrowing," said Littlejim. "But thank you."

"We will be happy to help you, in return for my visit here this summer," said Myron. "And a visit next year, I hope."

Nell was running up the path, followed by a tall mailman. "Littlejim, Mr. Hullinder needs to talk with you," she called.

"Morning, Littlejim," the mailman said, then tipped his leather cap to Myron. "You must be the visitor from off. Philadelphia, wasn't it? I've noticed the mail from there."

"I am," said Myron, shaking hands with him. "And today I go *off* again. To Philadelphia."

Turning back to Littlejim, Wil said, "Did your pa decide to sell the timber on that boundary in the Charl Ollis cove, over by the cemetery?"

"No," said Littlejim. "Papa says that is the best stand of timber on the place, our only virgin trees. He has been saving them because he says they will bring prime dollar."

"Do you mean that part of the land Mr. Houston sold the mineral rights for?" asked Myron, his face distorted with worry. Littlejim felt a black hole in the pit of his stomach as Myron asked the question.

"Yes," said Littlejim. "But he didn't sell the timber."

"Somebody is cutting those trees," said Wil. "I just passed one wagon on the road. And another was turning out of the cemetery road, both fully loaded."

"We have to *stop* them," shouted Littlejim.

"We did not sell the timber rights," said Myron.

"That may not matter," said Littlejim, unhooking the wagon attachments from Scott's harness.

Myron's gasp reflected his dawning awareness of what might be happening. "The contract indicated that the company could prepare the land to recover the minerals. Cutting the trees may be interpreted as clearing the land for mining operations to begin."

"Who's cutting Papa's trees?" shouted Nell. "We have to stop them."

"Nell, go into the house," said Littlejim sternly as he unharnessed Swain and led the horse away from the wagon. "Have Aunt Geneva fix us some dinner and hot coffee. Have it ready when we get back."

Throwing his body across Swain's back and struggling with the long wagon reins to bring himself upright, he shouted "You ride Scott" to Myron, who was struggling to wind the long reins around his arm before mounting the horse. As he mounted Scott's back,

Myron asked, "Why on earth are you asking her to cook?"

"It will keep her from following us. She might get hurt," replied Littlejim.

Fighting the long reins and struggling to stay mounted bareback, the boys urged Scott and Swain into a gallop, shouting and sliding down the hill path behind Wil Hullinder. Littlejim hoped they were not too late to save Papa's trees.

Chapter 23

"THEY'VE CUT PAPA'S best trees!" shouted Littlejim as they rode over the hill. Ahead, there was blue sky where the green of giant fir trees, seeming to touch the clouds, should have dominated the cove. As he stopped Swain to survey the damage, the breath left his body as if he had been struck in the chest.

"It looks like battlegrounds in Germany when I was there during the war," said Wil.

"This is criminal!" said Myron angrily.

Hardly believing what he saw, Littlejim walked Swain slowly among the huge stumps that had so recently been tall, stately balsams covering the undulating terrain of the cove. The fragrance of fir resin almost overwhelmed him, choking him with the sadness of the loss.

Shaking his head in disbelief, Myron followed slowly. Wil made his way down the hill directly below the pair. Calling back, he said, "I hear voices down here."

Turning his horse to follow Wil, Myron said, "I was

afraid some of the wording of the contract would be open to interpretation, but this sort of thing never occurred to me. I am sorry."

"Papa needed the money to take Mama to the hospital," said Littlejim. "He did not have time to ask for advice. Mr. Greene told me to warn Papa. My warning wasn't strong enough."

"It's criminal," repeated Myron.

As they approached a small pile of red clay, two heads appeared from a tunnel in the hillside.

"I guess you know you're trespassing," called one of the heads as the rest of the body appeared.

"If I am trespassing, so are you," said Littlejim. "My papa owns this land. And these trees."

"Your papa Bigjim Houston?" said the man.

"Yes sir," replied Littlejim. "What are you doing here? Papa sold the mineral rights, not the timber rights!"

"Had to prepare the land for mining, once we found minerals on it," said the man, spitting tobacco at Scott's hooves.

Wil rode forward. Looking down at the miner with a defiance that dared the man to spit at his horse, he said, "You needed to clear a patch about ten feet square to make this hole, not the whole boundary."

"We were told to clear the cove, then to prepare for our mining operations," said the second miner, coming out into the sunlight.

"Who told you to do that?" asked Myron.

"Dearborne Guinn," said the miner. "He is in charge of the whole operation on this Creek."

"Guinn!" Wil almost spat the word at the man. "And him a neighbor, too. Pick a time when a man's away, gone to the hospital with his sick wife, and steal his best timber. Then claim mineral rights give him leave to take everything the man has. Some neighbor! It's bad enough to have outlanders come in here and take everything, but for his neighbors to help them do it! What is this world coming to?"

Turning his horse abruptly away, Wil said, "Come on. We might as well get back to the house."

Anger and disappointment flooded over Littlejim, befuddling his mind. As he rode away he did not know which way he felt. One minute he wanted to lie on the ground, beat his fists against it, and cry. The next he wanted to ride back up the hill and hit the miners for taking his papa's best trees. Then as his face grew red with rage, he urged Swain into a trot, wishing he could find Mr. Guinn and—and—and....He did not know what he would do if he found Mr. Guinn.

"We have to let Papa know," said Littlejim. "We will have to send him a telegraph message."

"Or call him," said Myron, now alongside him. "The rail station has a telephone."

"If we call Papa, there's nothing he can do anyway. It will scare him. He has enough to do with Mama. I don't think anybody has ever made a telephone call to him."

"This must be settled in court. Perhaps a judge could decide if the contract is legal," said Myron.

"I don't think Papa has ever lawed anybody," said Littlejim. "He doesn't trust the court."

"He must do something," said Myron as they rode around the bend in the road to ford the creek.

Sitting across the water Littlejim could see two men on horseback. One of them was Guinn. Feeling his anger rise into his throat, Littlejim pushed his energy down his arms and into his fists clenched tightly on the reins. Facing down the class bully four years ago was different from facing a grown man in a fancy suit.

But he took a deep breath and urged Swain into the water without taking his eyes off the taller of the two men, the one whose eyes were hidden beneath his broad-brimmed hat. In his mind, he was willing the man to back up, to dismount, to do anything except sit with a smirk, chewing his cigar.

As he reined in Swain a few feet from the men, Littlejim exhaled to quiet his trembling and said quietly and firmly, "Why did you cut my papa's timber? You have no right."

"Good morning, Littlejim. Gentlemen," the man said as he tipped his hat and pulled a sheet of paper from his pocket. "Rights sold here in this contract, son. Signed and witnessed by you and this young"—he paused, raising one eyebrow—"lawyer. The contract states that we can prepare the land for prospecting and mining. That's all we're doing."

"Then the profits from the sale of the timber belong to Mr. Houston, I assume," said Myron.

"No sir," said Mr. Guinn. "Five percent of the profits from the sale of the minerals belong to him. Nothing more. Ain't nothing in this contract about his share from preparing the land for mining operations."

"Some neighbor you are," said Wil Hullinder. "We ought to run you out of this valley."

"Powerful folks down in Raleigh can help a mailman keep or lose his job," said Mr. Guinn. "Could be they know the bigwigs up in Washington who decide these things. I'd be careful, if I was you."

Wil continued to ride down the road toward the Houston house. "Some neighbor," he repeated.

Littlejim and Myron urged the horses around the men, without taking leave of them.

"Good day, Littlejim," Mr. Guinn called sarcastically.

For the first time in his life, Littlejim deliberately ignored an adult's acknowledgment. Lifting his head defiantly, he stiffened his back. This man who had stolen from his family would see before him the man of the Houston family, at least while Papa was away. The thief would not see the frightened boy Littlejim felt like inside, not if he could help it.

Chapter 24

"S IR," MYRON SAID to the stationmaster when they arrived at the railway station the following morning, "we need to use the telephone."

"Telephone's for railway business only," said the stationmaster.

"I need to speak with my father in Philadelphia about my ticket," said Myron, picking up a brochure from the desk. "I missed my train yesterday, and I have lost my ticket. Name's Farber. Myron Farber."

Checking his drawer hurriedly, the stationmaster said, "Farber? Philadelphia? Sorry, no tickets in the file."

"Then I will need to speak to my father in Philadelphia about the ticket," said Myron, looking over the brochure. "He will speak to his friend Mr. Norton about it. I believe that he has some position or other with the railroad."

"Mr. Norton? He is a friend of your father's?" said

the man, gathering papers to clean off his desk. "Yes, he does. He is president of this railroad. Your father is a friend of his?"

"I have heard him mention Mr. Norton many times, and his law firm represents several railroads. It could be another Mr. Norton, but…" Myron turned to leave. Littlejim hesitated, sensing that something was happening that he did not quite understand.

"Mr. Farber." The stationmaster's voice was suddenly welcoming. "Of course, if your father knows Mr. Norton, then your call becomes railroad business. Of course you may use the telephone. You understand, I'm sure. Shall I get the operator for you?"

"Thank you, sir. I'll tell my father how helpful you have been. He may have to return the call. May we wait here?" asked Myron, taking the chair behind the desk and picking up the phone.

"Of course," said the stationmaster. "You may use the office as long as you want to. I'll be out here working with the ticket agent." And he closed the door.

Littlejim had not quite followed the conversation. "Does your father really know the president of this railroad?" he asked, perplexed.

"Probably," said Myron, looking through the papers in his coat pockets. "He knows several railroad presidents. Mr. Norton *could* be one of them. I found his name on the brochure. My father's best friend is a Vernon Norton, a physician. I did not lie."

Littlejim was still confused.

"Look, Littlejim. I hate playing the big-city gent. I hate people who are insincere. But we needed to use the phone. It is the only phone in town. I played into the man's assumptions that all city people are likely to know railroad presidents."

"Why would he assume that?" asked Littlejim, still confused. "Does he think you are better somehow because you come from Philadelphia?"

"Perhaps," said Myron, shaking his head. "It's not fair but, you see, it's sort of the reverse of the assumptions outsiders bring to the mountains. Most of the people who visit here have the money to travel and many of them know influential people. Those with less money do not travel. The stationmaster has met people traveling here on vacation trips, people who live up to his expectations of what city folk are like, and so he assumes that because I came from"—he stopped and said the word with a simper—"Philadelphia, I certainly know presidents of railroads and other influential people. I played into his expectations so we could use his phone. Now I must call my father to ask him to call your father about the trees."

"You sure fooled me," said Littlejim. "But it must be much easier to have people think you are smart and modern and educated and that you know influential people than it is to have people think you are poor and ignorant and backward just because you live in the country, especially in the Appalachian Mountains—like your friend, Mr. Bradley thinks."

"He's no friend of mine. Never was, but he certainly is not my friend since he treated you so badly in his article," said Myron, giving the operator information between his statements to Littlejim. "I guess it is—easier, I mean—to make people think you are smart if you live someplace else. I never realized that we expect people to be a certain way because they live in a certain place, wear certain clothing, or look a certain way. I guess we all judge people based on standards which are unfair, don't you? We do it without realizing it." Pausing to listen, he turned his full attention to the phone call. "Oh, hello, Father. Yes, I'm fine. I've been delayed, and I need your help. Could you please call Mr. Houston in Statesville for me?"

Myron continued to talk to his father as Littlejim thought about judging people based on how people looked or where they lived. He remembered how often Mama had scolded him and Nell for laughing at the holler people, those who lived back in the steep, narrow valleys with little farmland, away from the Creek community. They were often unwashed; dressed poorly, like the sangers at the station that day; and whined when they spoke. Whenever they had come to Burleson's Store when he and Nell were there, they had stayed as far away from them as possible, and the few days each year that the holler children attended school, he had been careful to avoid talking to them or playing with them.

Now he wondered if he had been treating the holler children as he had been treated by Mr. Bradley. How he wished Mama were there for him to talk to about this. She would be able, he was sure, to help him sort out all the new thoughts he was having. She would help him to see what was right.

Myron's voice and a slap on the shoulder brought Littlejim's thoughts back to the railway station. "Father says he will call your papa right away. The train will be coming in an hour. Let's find something to eat. I'm starved."

"How about some of Mr. Westall's good hoop cheese and soda crackers?" suggested Littlejim, his mouth watering.

"Sounds like a perfect end to the summer," said Myron. "And Littlejim," he said, leading the way out to the platform, "I have had a wonderful summer."

"It has been a good summer for me, too," said Littlejim, wondering why he was suddenly so formal with this young man who had become such a good friend. There were so many things he wanted to say, but none of them could find their way to his lips. Suddenly he realized how much he would miss his friend when the train pulled away. Remembering how much he had not wanted Myron to come for the summer, he now thought how much he wished his friend did not have to go.

Chapter 25

AT TWILIGHT LITTLEJIM drove the wagon into the barn. He knew he should take time to care for the team, but then the special surprise he and Myron had planned for Aunt Geneva, Nell, and May would be ruined. Papa would be furious with him for neglecting the horses, especially since he had pushed them to move at top speed up the River Road. But the surprise could not wait. Finally he poured some corn into the trough, but left the other chores for later.

Hurrying up the path, he hoped Aunt Geneva had saved supper for him. He was starved, although the boys had eaten their fill of cheese and crackers at noonday. Then they had walked to the pharmacy, where Myron had order something called a soda in two tall glasses for them to drink through paper straws. The soda was sweet and tickled Littlejim's nose with its bubbles. Myron told him that everyone in Philadelphia drank sodas. Littlejim decided that if he lived there, he would have one of the sweet bubbly drinks every day.

During their meal the friends decided that Littlejim should take a surprise back for everyone to enjoy. At the hotel they ordered a quart of chocolate ice cream to be ready at three o'clock, then they purchased a block of ice and some sawdust to pack it in so that it would not melt on the long journey home.

As Myron boarded the train, he said, "If your father does not call by three o'clock, pick up the ice cream and hurry home as fast as you can. Tell Aunt Geneva thank you, and tell Nell that I will see her at the toy store in Philadelphia." Then he added, growing still and formal, "I hate to see the summer end. I shall miss you and your family."

Wondering why it was so difficult to say the words, Littlejim said, "I shall miss you, too." As the boys shook hands solemnly, Myron reached out to clasp Littlejim's shoulder in friendship. Then he ran for the train, to wave from the window as the black locomotive chugged out of the station and disappeared around the bend in the river. Littlejim wondered if Myron, leaving, could possibly feel as much of a sense of loss as he did, watching him leave. Loneliness, like an empty place on the wagon seat, had urged him to push the horses faster and faster until at last he was relieved to see the light of the kitchen window as he drove into the barnyard.

Now as he hurried through the barnyard gate carrying the precious container of ice cream, the melting block of ice dripping down the top of his boots, his loneliness seemed to vanish, and he smiled when he thought of Nell's reaction to the treat they had arranged. His spirits were lighter on the way home than they had been since he had seen the barren landscape where Papa's best trees had stood. He had also felt better when Papa did not call the station. Perhaps that meant Mama was well and would come home soon.

But it was Littlejim who was surprised. Aunt Zony's buggy was sitting in the yard. He was happy she would be sharing their ice cream treat.

"Nell! Aunt Geneva! May!" he called, opening the door into the kitchen. "I have a surprise for you from Myron."

He stopped and stood in the doorway. Bigjim was sitting at the table, an empty coffee cup in front of him, his shoulders drooping, his head in his hands. Tarp sat across the table. Aunt Geneva, her eyes red from crying, stood lightly touching his arm, comforting. Nell was holding May, both of them serious and silent.

"How's Mama?" he asked, fearful of hearing the answer even as he said the words. "Is she home?"

His heart felt as if it dropped to his toes when Aunt Geneva stepped toward him. Something had happened to Mama; he was sure when his papa said forlornly, "Gone. Gone."

Aunt Geneva stepped toward her nephew. Littlejim wanted to run away from the words he was afraid to hear, but instead Bigjim said, "Gone. My best trees. Gone."

Littlejim thought Bigjim meant the trees were gone, not Mama. But he had to be sure. "Mama? Where's Mama?" he asked.

Aunt Geneva spoke softly to him. "Your mama's getting well. Jim came home because she is getting better. Tarp told him about the trees when he arrived only a few minutes ago. He is taking that hard because he has just learned about the men cutting them." Littlejim almost smiled in relief.

"When will Mama be coming home?" he asked, oblivious to the icy water wetting his shirt and pants.

"Next week," said Nell, and May repeated, "Home. Home. Home," and giggled with delight.

"Gone," Bigjim repeated.

"They will grow back," insisted Tarp.

"Not in our lifetime," said Bigjim. "Not that you and I will ever see, nor my boy here. Mayhap trees that size will never grow again in these mountains."

"What are you dripping on the floor?" asked Nell. She moved closer to examine the canvas-wrapped bundle her brother was carrying.

"Jimmy," chided Aunt Geneva, "you are dripping water on my clean floor!"

"Oh, I forgot," he said. "Myron sent everyone a treat from town to say thank you for his visit. Now we can celebrate Mama's coming home, too."

"How can we celebrate at a time like this?" growled Bigjim. "My trees. My biggest trees. Gone." Littlejim was confused. He thought Papa should be happy that Mama was coming home, but then he remembered how proud Papa had been, as a lumberman, that he had saved one stand of large virgin firs long after other trees like his had been cut and sold. It made some sense. Mama was getting well, but his trees would never be there again.

"Jim," said Tarp in a determined voice, "I agree. Your trees are gone. You were cheated. That is an awful situation. The bare cove is an awful sight. I just came from a ride over there." Standing up, he took the bundle from Littlejim's hands and set it in the dishpan. "However, we have many things to be thankful for in this house this day. Things we *can* celebrate while we decide what to do about the trees. You have brought us news that your good wife, my cousin 'Trude, has come through the operation and will be home in a few days. Now your fine son has brought a gift from your guest to help us celebrate. We will enjoy this gift, then we will talk about ways to overcome the bad news. Right, Geneva?"

Opening the carton, Tarp exclaimed, "Why, that boy's made it all the way from town with chocolate ice cream! It's a mite soft, but it's still ice cream! Nell, bring some bowls and spoons, please."

Bigjim stood suddenly and walked out the door, but the others hardly noticed. Tarp passed the bowls of ice cream, and they savored the cold sweetness.

"It's every bit as good as that day we ate it at the hotel," said Nell, licking her spoon. "It's better than snow cream, even Mama's."

The door opened. Bigjim hung his hat on the peg beside the door and picked up the last bowl from the table. "Ain't much a man can do about the trees tonight."

Scooping the last bit from the carton and picking it up to allow the last drop to drain into his bowl, Bigjim walked to his accustomed place at the table and said, "Geneva, any coffee left?"

Winking at Littlejim as he scraped his bowl, Tarp said, "Fine sweet to end a day. Good news about Gertrude. Now I feel fortified to talk about more unpleasant business, like your trees."

"Mama says she can always sweeten Papa up with a goodie," whispered Nell. "She says he has a sweet tooth." Littlejim playfully kicked her foot under the table. It seemed that the ice cream *had* changed their papa's mood, or maybe taking time to eat the treat Myron had sent had given Papa time to think about what Tarp had said.

"When will Mama come home, Papa?" said Littlejim.

"Mr. Burleson's auty-mobile will bring some important visitors up the mountain next Thursday," said Bigjim. "Gertrude will ride with them. Zony will bring her up the Creek in her buggy."

"Isn't that good news?" said Tarp.

"Oh, yes," they all said together, and laughed heartily at the sound of their chorus.

"Time to do the dishes," said Aunt Geneva.

"Oh," said Tarp, standing and moving toward the hall door. "Jim, you and me, we have to talk about what we're going to do about the trees."

"Men," said Aunt Geneva. "Always have more important things to do—more important than the everyday things that keep the world moving, I guess. Get out of here. The children and I will take care of the really important things, like dishes."

Littlejim did not like being included in *the children,* so he drew himself up to his full height, sitting straight in the chair.

"Aunt Geneva, I am not a child," he said. Nell imitated his posture, opening her mouth to object also, but Bigjim slammed his spoon down on the table.

"You ain't much of a man either. A man takes care of his horses before he eats. A man knows a good team is his livelihood."

Jumping out of his chair, Littlejim headed toward the door. His father's long arm reached out to stop him.

"The horses are fed, curried, and stabled, son," said Bigjim, surprisingly gentle. "Sit back down."

Littlejim almost fell back into the chair. His father had used the voice he used when talking with his wife, not the father-to-son voice he usually used when he spoke to his son.

Tarp turned back from the hallway to say, "Are you ready, Jim? Littlejim? Come along."

His father nodded to Littlejim, indicating that he too was included in the serious conversation that would follow. Taking a deep breath to clear the swimmy-headed feeling his father's tone had created, he looked at Aunt Geneva, rose, and followed the older men into the front room.

Chapter 26

L ITTLEJIM LEFT THE KITCHEN and walked down the hall to the rarely used parlor the family called the front room. His father was stacking a small pile of kindling on one stick of firewood and lighting a match for a small fire to take the chill off the room. Then Bigjim took his usual chair in front of the fireplace, nodding toward Mama's chair for Tarp, leaving Littlejim no place to sit except on the leather couch with curved arms, located behind the older men.

Making a quick decision, Littlejim decided to stand beside the fireplace and lean against the wall, his shoulder resting against the edge of the mantel, facing the others. As he moved his back against the wall to find a more comfortable position, he suddenly realized he was tall enough to lean his arm on the mantel just like his father usually did. He grinned to himself. He had not realized how tall he had grown—not quite as tall as Bigjim, but then few men were. However, for the first time in appearance, at least, he *was* now a man.

"Jim," Tarp began, taking his knife and a small block of pine out of the pocket of his knee-length logging pants and beginning to whittle. "Jim, I believe that you have to find a way to fight the men who took your trees under false pretenses," he said. "You must be the one to do it because you are the first to feel the effects of outlanders finding out what riches we have here in these hills."

Bigjim hesitated a moment, stretched one long leg out so that he could reach deep into one of his side pockets, and pulled out a small block of white spruce. Taking his knife with its open blade where he had placed it on the hearth, he began to trace a thin line into the wood to outline his carving.

For a few minutes the two men sat carving in silence. "Gone," said Bigjim finally, as if trying to believe his own words. "The last stand of virgin timber on the Creek—gone, stolen, rustled, cut, and hauled God-only-knows where. I won't ever see any of those trees again. Trees I wasn't sure I would ever cut. I thought to save them for the boy here." He nodded toward Littlejim. "Or even for his children. Or theirs."

Littlejim was startled, surprised to learn that his father cared enough to save anything for him, especially his prized trees. Then he was surprised at the thought that he too would be a father someday, with children to whom he would leave things he treasured. He blinked hard, trying to deal with all the new thoughts at once.

He almost missed hearing Bigjim say, "Tarp, have you read the *Raleigh Democrat* this week?"

"No," said Tarp. "I read the *Star,* comes up the west mountains on the train. Why?"

"Read the *Democrat* while I was in Statesville with Gertrude," said Bigjim. "Seems some feller over there in Knoxville, Tennessee, is organizing a group to buy mountain land and make it available to everybody who wants to visit it; calls it a *national park,* like Galen told us about out west. What do you think about that?"

"Seems like the way we've always done it," said Tarp. "Unless a man's land is fenced, we have always used common grazing lands, share and share alike. Anybody who wants to visit it can walk all over these hills. Somebody might ask him his business. That's all."

Bigjim carved for a few minutes in silence. Then he said, shaking his head sadly, "Our young visitor told me that he has heard talk of the government using its power of eminent domain to condemn land the owners don't want to sell. Then the government can just take the land to do whatever they might with it."

"Don't seem right," said Tarp. "It would seem that in a democracy a man has a right to live on land his forefathers left to him with a deed and all."

"Lots of things don't seem right these days," said Bigjim. "It seems that the big boys up north have discovered what riches these hills have to offer. They seem bent on taking it from us. Everywhere a man turns, somebody's trying to steal what has belonged to his family for generations. Sometimes I wonder if we'll have anything left to leave our children when we're gone."

"Does make a man wonder," agreed Tarp.

The two men sat watching the small fire for a few minutes. Littlejim walked over to the table beside the door and picked up the latest edition of the *Star*. As the conversation continued, he glanced at the articles but could find nothing of interest. Folding the paper, he eased his body down to sit on the cold hearth, wincing because the fire had done little to warm the stones.

"According to the *Democrat,* some folks over in the Smokies have newsmen and writers from magazines all over the place," said Bigjim. "The article said they are writing all sorts of untruths about the people who live there."

"Untruths," said Tarp. "A lie is a lie. Just call it a *lie.*"

"Now, Tarp," said Bigjim, much to his son's surprise. "A lie has evil intent. The article did not say the writers had evil intent. It only said they made things worse than they were, wrote about the people being isolated since pre–Revolutionary War time, backwoodsmen, ignorant and living in the century past."

Tarp took out his pipe tobacco, tapped a small amount into his pipe, lit it, and took a few exploratory puffs, leaning back in his chair to savor the experience.

Then he spoke. "Writers are making mountain people sound ignorant and backward. One article I read in the *Star* said we have practically no contact with the world outside our local communities."

"Didn't they talk to people like Brother Galen, who has been all over the West and who even rode with Buffalo Bill?" said Bigjim. "I've heard him tell tales of the forests of Oregon and the deserts and the Indians of the Arizona territory, all places he has been. He even gave Zony her name. She's named for Arizona when it was still only a territory. Why, Buffalo Bill even tried to get him to go across the sea to Europe with his Wild West show. If he hadn't decided to come home and marry that pretty gal, I guess he would have met the queen of England."

"No, I guess they haven't talked to Galen," Tarp agreed. "I guess they could have talked to Cousin Harry, too. He was a clown for Barnum and Bailey's Circus, traveled all over the world. I wouldn't be surprised if he did meet the queen of England. Where is he now? Working for some Irishman up in Boston, last I heard."

"Yeah, some Kennedy feller up in Boston is the last word I had about him," Bigjim said. "Harry's the best distiller ever raised up in these parts. What with Prohibition being passed this year and all, I guess he is a valuable man to have in the business of making or selling whiskey, legal or illegal. I reckon he can make more money bootlegging in the city than he can here in these hills, don't you?"

Tarp nodded calmly while Littlejim watched his father continue to whittle, but he was startled to hear his father say that a member of his family might be involved in something illegal, and surprised to see no reaction from his papa or Tarp as they discussed the possibility.

"Don't have to go to Boston or out west to talk to men who deal with the outside world," Bigjim went on. "Any day, these newspaper fellers could talk to any of us timbermen, or the mill owners who deal with outside markets on a regular basis."

"Or the farmers like me. We take our produce and stock to the Piedmont markets twice a year. Or the families from here on the Creek who ride the train down the mountain to Tennessee to visit their relates," said Tarp, puffing on his pipe.

"But maybe the writers don't see those people because they're looking for something else," said Littlejim. "Like the travel writer from the magazine who did not see anyone at the train station that day except the 'sangers. He wrote about them as if everyone here is like they are. Then he wrote something untrue about me and made the picture look as if I were ignorant."

Both men looked at him, their eyebrows arched. "Wrote about you?" said Tarp. "You were in a magazine? Why didn't you tell us?"

"Son, what are you hiding from me this time?" said Bigjim, hands freezing as he stopped carving and leaned forward to look intently at his son.

Chapter 27

Do you remember when that travel writer came to Spruce Pine early this summer, the one Myron and I met at the train?" asked Littlejim.

Each of the men nodded in agreement as the boy told of his embarrassment when his photo had appeared in the magazine and explained how the writer had ridiculed the family on the platform that day.

When Littlejim had finished his explanation, Bigjim placed both his knife and his block of wood on the hearth, lifted his head, and pointed one long finger at his son. "This has to stop," he said loudly and firmly. Not knowing what to expect, Littlejim drew back against the wall. "No outlander is going to treat my son like dirt," he heard his father say.

Startled by his father's vigorous support, he protested, "But Papa, I've already written a letter to the magazine."

"No, I mean the outlanders coming into our homes,

our lands, and making us out to be fools in front of the rest of the world." Bigjim was angry, his words exploding from his lips. "That writer was only one part of it. Shysters beating me out of my trees is another. We have to take a stand!"

Tarp stopped whittling and looked at Bigjim intently. "What are you proposing we do?" asked Tarp.

Rising to pace back and forth, Bigjim said, "I think we'll begin by writing a letter to Myron's father in Philadelphia. He did say his father is a lawyer, didn't he, son?"

"Attorney-at-law," said Littlejim, pleased with himself that he knew the terminology.

"What shall we write?" asked Tarp. "How do we ask for his help?"

Bigjim drew himself up to his full height. "My son here is a *champion* writer. Even the *Star* said so. He will help us write a fine letter."

Littlejim's jaw dropped and his eyes widened. His father was praising him. He never thought, to use Aunt Geneva's favorite expression, he would live to see the day.

"Son, get your paper and pen. We are going to write a letter," said Bigjim. Tarp sat startled, as surprised as his nephew to hear words of praise for the boy.

"Well, son, are you froze to the floor?" Bigjim asked.

Littlejim nodded his head and rose awkwardly, trying to get his arms and legs to move in tandem, so surprised that he was not sure if he could make them work to walk across the floor. Then his surprise turned to joy, and he bounded up the stairs to the sleeping loft, taking three steps at a time. Scrambling around in his metal box, which guarded his precious paper and pencils, he found the best sheet of paper he owned. But he had no pens, only one pencil and one square pink eraser.

Remembering Mama's writing box in the dining room cupboard, Littlejim hurried to find her wooden quill, pen nubs, and ink, and he met Nell coming from the kitchen.

"Littlejim, you would wake the dead," she said. "Aunt Geneva just got May to sleep. What are you doing?"

"We"—he emphasized the word—"are going to write a very important letter to Myron's father to ask for his help about the trees. Where are Mama's pens?"

"She took some of them to the hospital," said Nell. "I think there's one in the box." Searching through the cupboard, she finally held up a new pen nub, attached to a worn quill with teeth marks on the sides, and a bottle of dark black ink. "Tell him I will come to Philadelphia to visit the toy store one day soon."

"Oh, Nell," said Littlejim impatiently. "We are writing about important things."

"Well, important things include Aunt Geneva, Mama, May, and me, too," she said.

"I know that," said Littlejim, growing more impatient. "But right now we have to get this letter written. I will add your greetings to Myron at the end. All right?"

"Good," said Nell. "And don't forget the toy store."

"Girls!" said Littlejim under his breath as he closed the door and ran back down the hall.

When he was settled on the couch in the parlor, the lamp table pulled in front of him and the light of the kerosene lamp falling on the paper, Littlejim dipped his pen into the ink.

"We will write a fine letter," said Bigjim. "And you will take it to put it on the first train to Philadelphia."

But what Bigjim and Tarp did not know was that the next morning Littlejim rose long before sunup, built a fire in the kitchen range before the rest of the family awoke, and placed the coffeepot to boil on the woodstove. Then he lighted the lamp, poured himself a cup of coffee, and began to compose another letter to his friend Myron, explaining what had happened about the trees since his departure and what was happening to other mountain residents. At the end he asked Myron for suggestions about ways one lone boy in a small valley in the mountains could help his father and the other people who were losing their trees and land to outsiders. Littlejim often smiled when he remembered how he had hated for Myron to come and how much he missed his friend when he was gone. He hoped to hear news of

Myron and his school experiences almost as much as he hoped for help for his papa.

Both letters were carried in Littlejim's pocket as he rode Scott's back to the train station to mail them to Philadelphia. The rhythm of Scott's hooves caused his thoughts to drift off into his dreams, so long neglected. As he thought about sitting in a great university surrounded by books, he realized that, even when Mama was so ill, he could find moments of happiness in reading or writing. Dreaming about what the future might hold for him, he decided that yes, he would learn to fly an aeroplane, but whatever he did would involve writing. Maybe he would write about aeroplanes. Yes, that would be a fine thing to do, or so he thought.

But right now he hoped that the words he had written would bring information about helping Bigjim and others on the Creek. That was what he most wished for his words to do just now.

Then day after day when Littlejim saw Wil Hullinder ride up the Creek Road, he stopped his chores to run over to meet the mailman, hoping that he carried a letter from Myron or his father, and wishing he also had a letter from the *Star*. Often the tall, friendly mailman laughed as he told the boy that Bigjim had already met him on the road.

Chapter 28

THERE WAS SO MUCH to be done before Mama came home that Littlejim and Nell were busy from morning until night. Aunt Geneva insisted that the bed be taken apart. Then the parts of the bed, the washstand, and the chairs in Mama's room were carried outdoors, washed with soap and water, and left to dry in the sun. Littlejim threw the feather beds across the clothesline, where Nell and May beat them with sticks to fluff and dust them.

Then they opened the seams of the straw tick and stuffed fresh straw into the large sack until it was ready to burst at the seams. As Littlejim and Nell held the opening, Aunt Geneva sewed it tightly so that no straw could peep through it as it supported the feather beds on which Mama would lie when she came home.

The trio carried everything, now clean and fresh, to wait on the porch while Littlejim carried pail after pail of water from the springhouse so that Aunt Geneva,

Aunt Zony, her daughter Helen, and the hired girl could scrub the floors with sand until they looked like new wood.

As the women cleaned the floors, Littlejim tended the fire under the big black wash pot where the bed linens were boiled to make them white and clean. Using a paddle much larger than she was, Nell and Littlejim took turns stirring the pot and added Mama's lye soap to wash the linens clean and white. May ran back and forth carrying small sticks of firewood from the stack Littlejim had made nearby to keep the fire going all day.

When the linens were hung on the line to dry, everyone could rest and enjoy bowls of Aunt Geneva's hot potato soup with tiny pieces of ham floating in it. Spreading a tablecloth on the floor of the porch, Aunt Geneva invited them to sit on the front steps and enjoy their soup and corn bread in the fresh air.

"We'll have our dinner-on-the-ground, even if we eat it on the porch," she said, laughing happily. "Now, Nell and Littlejim, it is up to us to have our all-day singing, too. You can help me."

As she and Aunt Zony began to sing, "Lolly-too-dum, too-dum. Lolly-too-dum, day," Aunt Geneva dipped bowls full of soup with the ladle and cut the corn bread into wedges. May joined them in her loudest voice, slightly off pitch. Littlejim, Helen, and Nell almost fell over laughing. Delighted with the attention from the older children, May smiled and sang more loudly, making her voice even more off pitch. Finally everyone was laughing so hard that Aunt Geneva placed the bowl she was filling on the top step and joined in the merriment.

"I guess we'll have our all-day singing, then we'll have dinner-on-the-porch, don't you?" she asked happily, a question that sent the children into fits of laughter again.

"Dinner-on-the-porch," repeated Nell, falling off the step as she began to laugh again.

"I think we are almost as pickled as those chickens on the joy that Gertrude is coming home, don't you?" said Aunt Geneva, passing the corn bread.

At last the laughter subsided and the group grew quiet as they planned for Mama's arrival the following day.

"We will line the path to the house with all our flutter mills," said Nell. "Won't we, Littlejim?"

"I will send some phlox in a vase to brighten her room," said Aunt Zony.

May, who had been chasing a sparrow back and forth across the yard, stopped to pick one of Mama's sweet williams and bring it to Nell.

"For Mama," she said, smiling. "Fl'rs."

When they had finished eating, the girls began chasing one another around the yard, hiding behind the box-woods that formed a border near the fence. A few days ago Littlejim would have joined in the chase, but this day he sat watching, feeling infinitely old. Turning to Aunt Zony, he said, "Do you think—?"

His sentence was interrupted by shouts from the road below the embankment.

"An auty-mobile! A red one!" shouted Nell. "It's coming up the road. Come, Littlejim. Come look!"

Running to the small ledge of stones at the roof of the springhouse, which gave him a view of the entire road from the curve to the path leading to his own front yard, Littlejim leaned forward. Chugging up the road was a red auty-mobile with a yellow sign on its roof. As it turned the curve in the road, he could see a sign on the side that read PINES HACK COMPANY. HIRED CONVEYANCE BY THE HOUR OR BY THE MILE.

Myron had pointed out the hired cars in town when they had met the travel writer there, explaining that in the city they were sometimes called taxicabs because the distance of each trip was measured by a taximeter, a small counter near the driver. To have an automobile of any sort driving up the Creek Road was an event, but Littlejim, in his wildest dreams, had never imagined a real hack driving right up the road near his house.

The hack chugged around the bend and slowed to a stop near the path up the hill to the Houston house. Taking long steps but trying not to show his excitement that such a marvelous vehicle was stopping at his house, Littlejim hurried across the yard to the path. In two long leaps he reached the bottom of the steps just as the back door of the hack opened and a man who looked vaguely familiar stepped out and looked around him.

Turning to the driver, the man said, "Wait until I can speak with Mr. Houston."

The driver answered, but Littlejim could not hear his words. Turning around, the man offered his hand to Littlejim. "I am Donald Farber of Farber, Farber, and Palmer, Philadelphia. I am representing Mr. Myron Farber, Sr., my brother and partner, here to see Mr. James M. Houston. Do you know where I could find him?"

Chapter 29

THE EXPRESSION on the new Mr. Farber's face as he approached the house, with all the furnishings from Mama's room all over the porch and the noonday dinner dishes sitting on the floor, told Littlejim that their visitor had read articles describing "Hill-billie" homes in the big-city magazines like Mr. Bradley's. Chuckling, the boy hastened to explain that the house was in the midst of a grand cleaning because Mama would come home from the hospital tomorrow. He could almost see relief spread over the man's face as he realized that the appearance of the yard and porch was not typical.

When Bigjim and Tarp arrived, hurriedly summoned from the woods after Littlejim had flung his long legs across Scott's back and ridden to their cutting site, Mr. Farber seemed more at ease with the men. Covered with sawdust and shavings, the two men hardly noticed the hack waiting at the roadside in front of the house.

Barely taking time to wash the evidence of their day in the woods from hands and faces, they led the way to the parlor to sit on the leather couch with curved arms, used only on special occasions.

To his great surprise, Littlejim was allowed to sit in the front room as the men discussed the situation and sought possible solutions.

"My trees can't be brought back," said Bigjim sadly.

"But we can seek compensation, and we can stop this from happening to your neighbors," explained Mr. Farber.

"Dearborne has approached almost everyone on the Creek," explained Tarp. "But Jim's experience has scared most of them. Nobody's selling rights to anything since Jim's trees were stolen."

"They expected that and took the most valuable thing here first, Mr. Houston's trees," said Mr. Farber. "The problem was that the contract was so broadly worded that it was open to any interpretation they wanted to give it, including cutting your timber as preparation for mining operations. That was intentional. However, it is stretching the word *preparation* to allow for cutting five acres of virgin forest to dig one mine shaft measuring about eight feet square." His voice scoffed at the absurdity of the interpretation. "A legal contract in your favor would have been very specific about such details."

"Young Farber read it," said Bigjim. "And he was

worried that his knowledge was not broad enough. He tried."

"Yes, his father and I were a bit upset that he had assumed more knowledge than he has at his level in the school of law."

"He was trying to help us," said Bigjim, in what Littlejim could see was an attempt to defend Myron's efforts. The boy could hardly understand the surprising words coming from his father, but he was happy to have him change for, as the boy saw it, the better.

"Our next step is to go to the county seat and have a judge provide us with the legal papers we need," said Mr. Farber. "My taxicab is waiting at the roadside."

"My sister, Zony, is a magistrate," said Bigjim. Littlejim had forgotten that his aunt could act as a judge in matters of local interest, but he was happy to be reminded because he knew she would help them.

"Best not to have a member of the family or anyone related to write the papers," said Mr. Farber. "We can take my taxicab to the county seat to see a circuit judge."

Littlejim watched his father's eyes widen as if to ask Tarp where the money was coming from to pay for a hack, but Mr. Farber said, "My brother has given me instructions to take care of this matter, at the expense of the trust fund set up for your defense or at his personal expense, to see that justice is done. Gentlemen, after you." He made a little bow and hurriedly led them out to the porch as if to prevent further conversation at the time.

As they started down the steps, Bigjim hesitated again, looking down at his dirty overalls and muddy logging boots at the same moment Tarp walked out into the yard to dust the wood shavings from his shirt.

"I will understand if you would like to change into more suitable clothing, gentlemen. Feel free. I will wait in the cab for you," said Mr. Farber. "Young Jim, would you like to visit with me while I wait?"

Littlejim had so many questions he wanted to ask the man from the city that he hardly knew where to start. But as they walked down the path to the road, Mr. Farber asked him what he liked to read, and the pair discussed books until they reached the taxicab.

"Myron tells me you like the work of Jules Verne," said Mr. Farber. "He tells me that you are one of the visionaries who believe that man will one day move off this earth to explore the moon. How does a young man from this remote place form such revolutionary ideas?"

"I read," said Littlejim, wondering how on earth a grown man would not know the answer to such a question without asking.

"And what do you read to know so much about the world?" asked Mr. Farber, not unkindly, but with a great deal of interest in the answer, or so Littlejim thought.

"Books. The *Kansas City Star.* The *Raleigh Democrat,* sometimes. Even the *New York Times,* when Aunt Zony loans it to me. She loans me magazines, too. And I think. Sometimes I have gone to market in the towns down in the Piedmont with Papa. I guess people here know a great deal about the outside world, even though people in the outside world know very little about us, and what they know is sometimes not true."

By the time he had finished answering Mr. Farber, Littlejim was smarting from the memory of his humiliation in the article written by the travel writer.

"*Touché,* my young friend," said Mr. Farber, smiling. "And you are as articulate as Myron said you were. That will serve you well. Perhaps you should think about law school some day."

Littlejim's thoughts were spinning with Mr. Farber's words when the man placed his valise on the trunk of the hack and opened it. "Well, young Jim," the man said, pulling out a newspaper. "I think a great many people will know what happened to your father and what is happening to your way of life, because of you and your sizable writing abilities."

"Yes, I won—," Littlejim began to explain, but Mr. Farber interrupted him, handing the newspaper to his young companion.

"I know all about your essay," said Mr. Farber. "Fine job. Myron shared it with me, but I am talking about your eloquent letter here in the *Philadelphia Inquirer.*"

"In the what?" Littlejim almost shouted. "I didn't write—"

Mr. Farber stopped him. "Your letter about what is

happening to the Appalachian people and their way of life has caused quite a stir in the city. Myron's father and I were trying to decide if we could help in this case, given our schedules, when the letter appeared. Your mention of our firm as a postscript resulted in an overwhelming number of calls praising us for coming to your aid and offering donations to cover the legal fees to defend your father's claim. The donations will cover your case all the way to the Supreme Court if necessary."

"But I wrote to Myron," Littlejim began again. Then as Mr. Farber replied with further explanations, the boy began to understand what had happened. He remembered Myron's persuasive skills demonstrated that day in the railroad station, and a broad smile warmed his face as he realized how his letter had reached a large city newspaper.

"Thank you, my friend," he whispered softly, seeing in his mind a picture of Myron waving from the train that last day of his visit.

Mr. Farber closed the valise. "You may keep that copy," he said, opening the trunk of the hack. "I have strict orders not to mention the article to your father until you are ready to tell him. All right? Now walk around here, young man." He took a large package wrapped in brown paper from the trunk and handed it to Littlejim. "A gift from my nephew," he said. "He thought you might enjoy this."

"What is it?" asked Littlejim, overwhelmed that his

friend would send him a gift, especially so large a package.

"Look at it," said Mr. Farber as Littlejim took out his pocketknife and cut the brown twine encircling the package.

Carefully unfolding the paper, Littlejim could see the spines of several books, two of which had Jules Verne's name on them. Lifting them out, he could see there were several more he had never heard of: *Winesburg, Ohio* by Sherwood Anderson, *The Age of Innocence* by Edith Wharton, and *The Mysterious Affair at Styles* by Agatha Christie—all the new books he had read about in the *New York Times.* The last book in the box was *The Complete Drawings of Leonardo da Vinci*—a copy of his very own—the book he had used to build his wonderful flying machine almost two years ago.

The boy's mouth slowly spread into a delighted grin as he said, "Please tell Myron I send thanks to him. I am much obliged for his kind gifts. I will write him a letter. Another letter."

A short while later, it was with only a small feeling of envy that Littlejim watched his father and Tarp, now dressed in their Sunday-finest clothing, drive away in the hack to see a judge in the county seat, almost fifteen miles away. He was so eager to begin reading his new books that helping his aunts reconstruct Mama's room, so clean that it looked new, seemed to take forever. But he was sure Mama would feel very welcome when she returned to her home tomorrow.

When his chores were done and supper was finished, Littlejim settled down near the kerosene lamp, now lit, for the days were getting shorter and the evening earlier, to begin to read when Nell came in carrying the lantern.

"Littlejim, we must make sure the fluttermills are ready for Mama tomorrow. Come with me," she urged, tugging at his sleeve.

As much as he wanted to continue exploring his new books, especially the da Vinci one, Mama would be coming home tomorrow, and he wanted to make sure she felt welcome. His new books would have to wait.

So, with Littlejim carrying the lantern low so that Nell could see, the pair lined the path to the house with the fluttermills to welcome Mama home when she arrived the following day.

Chapter 30

MOVING QUIETLY because, for the first time in anyone's memory, Bigjim slept beyond sunrise, Aunt Geneva and the children had preparations for Mama's arrival well underway when Aunt Zony brought a pretty new flowered coverlet, woven by one of her former students, to brighten Mama's bed, saying, "I will meet Gertrude at Burleson's Store. Let Jim sleep. He was planning to go for her, but I can take the buggy."

Littlejim had heard his father, Tarp, and their visitor from Philadelphia arrive late the previous night as the taxicab chugged through the night silence of the Creek community. After making his way down the narrow staircase, he had asked his father for details of the trip to the county seat, only to be told that the morning would be soon enough for details. Then Bigjim had blown out the lamp and gone to bed.

Before breakfast the children ran outside to admire their fluttermills lining the grass-covered driveway into the barn. They stood in the side yard where visitors parked their buggies. In the bright light of early autumn, the blades of the fluttermills turned in the breeze, making the soft colors that Nell had so carefully applied dance and move in so many rhythms that the yard seemed to be alive with color.

May ran around the yard picking every flower in sight and arranging them haphazardly on the steps. "For Mama," she said with each new addition to her arrangement. Aunt Geneva came to the porch every few minutes to remind them that Papa slept just inside the open window, despite the noise and laughter outside.

Littlejim was uprighting one of the fluttermills knocked down by the wind when Bigjim came around the side of the house from the kitchen, yawning and stretching. Aunt Geneva followed with a cup of coffee and, when he was seated in his rocking chair, handed it to him.

Looking up at his father, Littlejim asked, "What happened with the judge?"

"You will join us later when we discuss it. Right now we need to get ready for your mother," Bigjim answered. "I should have been in Plumtree to meet her."

"I am sure she will understand that you had to take care of the loss of your trees," said Aunt Geneva. "Zony will meet her and bring her home."

After drinking his coffee in silence, Bigjim walked down the steps and followed the path lined with fluttermills, shaking his head all the way. Turning to walk back to the house, Littlejim saw that his father continued to shake his head, but he was smiling—not the wide, happy smile of Uncle Bob or even the nose-wrinkling grin of Tarp, but they could clearly see that it was a smile that lifted the sides of his mustache as his brown eyes caught the light of the sun.

"It's a plumb pretty sight," he said. "I'll allow it's a *plumb pretty* sight! It's a fittin' sight to welcome 'Trude home."

Littlejim could not remember ever having seen his father's face wear so pleasant an expression, and the words were the happiest he could ever remember hearing his father speak. Surely having Mama come home today had brought great happiness to each member of the family, even to Bigjim.

Then Littlejim had a strange new thought that he did not understand. He thought that Mama's homecoming brought more happiness to his usually dour father than to anyone else, no matter how much they all loved Mama. He had never thought about his parents loving each other, but maybe Papa loved Mama as much as their children did. Maybe more.

May ran to Bigjim, who scooped her up into his arms as he called, "Nell, Littlejim, come here! Look." Pointing his long finger toward the sky, he said, "An eagle, come to welcome 'Trude home. I thought such great birds had disappeared from these lands forever. That's a good sign."

The quartet stood watching in silence as the great bird soared above them, but soon their silence was broken by the sound of an automobile engine chugging up the road. The red taxicab rounded the curve.

Bigjim sat May down on the ground, with a warning to all of them: "Stay up here on the bank. Don't follow me. Mind what I say."

Littlejim's feet itched to follow his father, but he knew that Bigjim meant to be obeyed. Walking as close to the edge of the embankment as he dared allowed him to see through the car's small rear window. Another tall man wearing a hat was riding in the backseat of the taxicab. The men had been talking for a few moments when the sound of a horse's hooves came from the distance and Aunt Zony's buggy came into view. Nell and May ran across the yard and down the hill to the springhouse, where they could wave to Mama as the buggy approached.

Littlejim felt his throat grow tight and his eyes fill with tears. Until that moment he had not realized *just* how much he had wanted Mama to come home. Or how much he had feared she would not. He stood very still until the feeling passed, then he ran across the yard to the barn driveway, where he could walk beside the buggy as it passed through the fluttermills on its way to the house.

As the buggy came slowly up the hill, Mama waved to him and smiled happily. When she saw the fluttermills, she smiled and clapped her hands like a small

child. By the time Aunt Zony had stopped the buggy, Bigjim and his visitors had joined the children at its side.

The girls hurried to hug Mama as Bigjim lifted her from the high seat and stood holding her in his arms. After gently helping her to stand on the ground, their father gave each child a moment to greet Mama. She smiled at them and said, "The best homecoming in the world, this is. All the wonder of fluttermills; so many of them I've never seen! Oh, thank you."

Mama's face was beaming, reflecting the joy her children felt in having made her feel so welcome. Then she looked at the two men standing at the gate. "And we have visitors, too. Who are our visitors, James?"

"Mr. Farber, Myron's uncle from Philadelphia, and this is Mr. Sparks, the good sheriff of our county," said Bigjim, nodding to the men. "And *this* is Mrs. Houston. Gertrude, my wife."

The two men doffed their hats as Mama looked up at Bigjim in alarm. "Why are we being visited by the sheriff, James?"

"Some business about the trees," said Bigjim hurriedly, his jaw stiffening. "Nothing for you to worry about. Your first concern is to get well. Are you strong enough to walk to the house, or shall I carry you?"

"James," Mama chided her husband. "A baby I am not. I will walk."

But Littlejim noticed that she did not decline her husband's offer of a strong arm for support.

Chapter 31

WHEN MAMA HAD RESTED and eaten the chicken soup Aunt Geneva made for her, Littlejim, Nell, and May went in to visit. May tumbled over to bring her head to rest on Mama's feet, stuck her thumb in her mouth, and began to hum to herself. A few minutes later, she was fast asleep.

"Mama, are you well?" asked Nell.

"The doctor says I'm—"

Bigjim's voice interrupted her. "I need the boy to go help me for a while. Do you need him here?"

Mama smiled at her tall husband. "He is yours for the rest of the day, James, but come nightfall I would like him safely home again. He can sit here and read to me."

As Littlejim and his father walked down the path toward the taxicab, Littlejim asked, "Are we going to ride in the taxi, Papa?"

"Farber says it's the best way. We're going to see

Dearborne Guinn. I didn't see it best to worry your mama with such details," said Bigjim. "I thought you should be a part of serving the papers on him. We're taking the law to serve them."

Littlejim's heart took a leap. His father was including him in the most important business his family had ever been involved in, as far as he knew. He felt taller than Spear Tops Mountain as he opened the front door and moved across the seat to allow his father to sit beside him.

Turning his neck uncomfortably to acknowledge his father's introduction to the sheriff, Littlejim caught his knee on the stick worked by the driver to make the car go forward. But he almost forgot the pain when the wind began to blow his hair as they moved down the road at a faster pace than the boy had ever ridden, even on Uncle Bob's little roan mare. It was amazing just how fast an auty-mobile could carry them. The trees and houses seemed to fly by as he waved to friends and neighbors standing gazing in awe at the red machine moving so fast down their road.

At the River Road the taxicab turned south and forded the river, chugging its way up the hill on a road hardly more than a path cut into the hillside. At the edge of a forest, the driver stopped and the men got out.

"You walk behind us," said Bigjim to his son. "I want you to be out of danger if he starts shooting."

Littlejim had had no idea that the situation was dangerous. "I thought we were here to serve papers. I didn't know that we might be involved in a shooting," he whispered.

"Unlikely," said the sheriff. "But you stay back anyway."

He watched as the men stepped single file into the low growth of rhododendron and pine. Littlejim followed, a few steps behind the others. He could hear the *chop, chop* of axes preparing to fell trees and the *skurr, skurr* of the saws eating their way through the tree trunks that would become fallen logs in a few minutes.

As they neared the clearing, Bigjim stood by to allow the sheriff and Mr. Farber to walk in first, but when Littlejim started to pass, he held out his arm. "No farther," he said. Littlejim opened his mouth to protest, but decided against it.

He watched quietly as the sheriff walked up to the man Littlejim recognized from that horrible day when Papa's cove of firs was decimated, his beautiful trees cut and carried away by strangers.

Listening carefully, he could hear the sheriff say quietly and forcefully, "This summons means you will appear in Judge Braswell's court one week from today to explain your reasons for *stealing*"—he emphasized the word—"Mr. Houston's stand of timber. Mr. Farber, an attorney, is witness that you have received this notice to appear in court."

And handing the paper to Mr. Guinn, the sheriff turned and walked back toward Littlejim and his papa, followed closely by Mr. Farber. Dearborne Guinn looked as surprised as if someone had slapped him, a thought that made Littlejim smile. He thought he might like to be the person to do that chore.

On the way back up the Creek Road, the older men were jubilant, laughing and talking loudly about the changes that were coming to the mountain communities. Occasionally the sheriff would remind them that mountaineers would need to be ever on their guard against outlanders' attempts to steal their land and timber. "The old saying 'A man's word is as good as his bond' means something here in these hills, but I hear it's just so many words most places. We can't count on outsiders, so we must be wary."

"But," Littlejim reminded him, eager to enter the conversation, "Mr. Guinn is not an outsider. He lives down the river."

"A thief is a thief, wherever he lives," said the sheriff. "We have thieves here, too. It just seems that outsiders don't live by the same rules the *men* here live by."

"That is probably true," said Mr. Farber. "The rules here seem to belong to a much earlier time, a time when people depended on one another. The life here seems to belong to colonial America more than it does to the twentieth century."

"Now look here," protested the sheriff. "I am tired of my people being called backward just because they don't have city ways. You won't find any better people than we have here in these hills!"

"No offense intended," said Mr. Farber. "In fact, I meant to compliment your culture. The colonial culture is that of Washington and Jefferson, the people who helped found this country, the laws of which have stood the test of time."

"I hate to see the old ways change," sighed Bigjim. "The world was easier to understand when I was a boy."

"But admit it, Jim," said the sheriff, slapping Bigjim on the back. "The trip we have just taken would have taken us all day on horseback. And here we are, back before sundown. Now you won't have to miss another day in the woods until court adjourns next week. Used to be, visiting every community in the county took me a week away from home. Now I can make almost any place in the county and be home for supper. The modrun"—Littlejim smiled at the mispronunciation—"world can't be all bad if it gets me home for some of Maude's hot corn bread every night."

"Speaking of supper," said Bigjim, smiling an unaccustomed smile. "Will you all stay to supper? I'm sure Geneva can water down the broth, and if she can't, we'll hang you on a nail and talk good to you."

Mr. Farber looked perplexed. "Oh, James, I wouldn't

want to put you out. Mrs. Franklin is expecting us at the boardinghouse, but exactly what did you mean by your invitation?"

It was Bigjim's turn to look perplexed. Littlejim realized that his father had no idea how to explain his jest to an outsider.

Turning to the men sitting in the backseat, Littlejim said, "I think that *watering down the broth* means that you are welcome, no matter how little we have for supper. And if we have nothing, not even a chair to offer, we will hang you on a nail on the wall, supported by your suspenders so you can rest, and we will give you all we have, an evening of good talk. In other words, you are welcome at our house to share what we have."

"Couldn't have said it better," offered the sheriff.

Bigjim nodded in agreement, still not quite sure why the visitor had failed to understand. "You are much obliged," he repeated.

"Perhaps I will take you up on that invitation later, but my plans for the days before the session opens include a bit of trout fishing along with my preparations for the case," said Mr. Farber.

"Now there is something I can do to repay my obligation to you," said Bigjim. "Nothing Gertrude likes more than trout. I could catch her a mess of them. Would you like to go early tomorrow morning?"

Littlejim's mouth fell open in surprise, but he quickly closed it and looked straight ahead, smiling. His father was going to take a day off and go fishing. He could hardly wait to tell Mama.

Later that night, as he sat in the chair beside her bed, Littlejim took out the page from the Philadelphia newspaper and shared the letter he had written with Mama. As he finished reading the letter, she reached out to take his hand.

"My fine son, the scholar, you have truly brought honor to our home this day. Such a fine letter, explaining your papa's problems and the problems faced by our mountain people. Your letter would turn the heart of the hardest man, and he would want to help us. And what a fine thing for Myron to do, to send your letter to the newspaper. It is a fine thing you have done."

Littlejim smiled and squeezed Mama's hand gently, then heard the door hinge creak and looked up to see Bigjim step back into the shadows and disappear.

Chapter 32

THE SHADOW OF THE Spear Tops darkened the valley, leaving only the edge of the ridge behind the house bathed in sunlight as Littlejim and his father waved to the riders in the taxicab and climbed the steep path into the yard.

Littlejim felt tall and strong as he walked beside his father. This was a day he would long remember, for Bigjim had allowed him to be a part of—no, he had *included* his son in—the business of the men of the family. Even if he did not say the words, his father had openly demonstrated, in the company of men he respected, that he included his son as another man.

Littlejim stood taller when he remembered his part in Mr. Farber's visit to help them to see that justice was done. He had yet to decide if he would tell his father or not. Then he remembered that Papa could have been listening as he read the letter to Mama. Maybe Papa already knew.

It was all Littlejim could do not to swagger as he approached the front porch, but his father looked up at the sunlit mountaintop above them and said, "Chores. The stock have to be tended before we can eat. A man has to take care of his livestock. They are his livelihood. Fetch some corn and fodder. See to the cows and pigs. I will see to the horses. Then we can eat supper. Milking can wait for lantern light."

Littlejim's heart leaped. His father had spoken to him like a partner, not a "no-good boy."

"Yes, sir," he said, stepping smartly down the path.

"Young buck," he heard Papa's voice say. "Well, if he isn't finally learning some manners. Will wonders never cease?"

As Littlejim carried an armload of fodder into the stall for Pink, Mama's favorite cow, he heard his papa say, "Someone's already seen to the milking."

The pair did not speak again as they took care of their tasks in the barn, but Littlejim noticed that Bigjim waited for him to walk to the house for supper. As they washed their faces and combed their hair at the washbasin on the porch, Nell came out to hug Bigjim, jumping up and down.

"What on earth is wrong with you, Nellie? You look like a limberjack, dancing every which way!" said Bigjim as his son thought he had heard his father speak more words that day than in all the rest of his life.

"Mama was well enough to eat all her supper," said

Nell. "And Littlejim has a letter from the *Kansas City Star*. We could hardly wait"—she paused, breathless— "but we didn't open it because it was addressed to you, Littlejim. Maybe you won the scholarship so you can go to the academy. Oh, I hope so! Come on, Littlejim. Hurry."

She tugged at her brother's sleeve, drawing him through the door, talking as fast as her mouth could move.

"What is this about a scholarship? Academy? What have you been hiding, boy?" Bigjim asked, his voice changing to the old scolding tone Littlejim had thought he had left behind forever.

"Don't you remember, Papa? We told you just before Mama became ill."

Bigjim nodded as Aunt Geneva placed in front of them some yellow squashes dipped in cornmeal and fried until they hid inside crispy succulent shells, the last of the summer's corn shaved off the cob and simmered in butter, some turnip greens cooked with ham, and a bowl of stewed tomatoes.

"We tried to keep it hot," said Aunt Geneva. "I hope it is still good."

As Bigjim asked the blessing, Littlejim was torn. He could hardly wait to taste the squashes in their corn shells, and he feared opening the letter in front of his papa.

"Why don't you eat before the food gets cold?" suggested Aunt Geneva. "And that will give you time to explain to your papa about the first letter." She and Nell sat across from each other at the end of the table, near the door to hear if Mama called.

Picking up his fork, Littlejim reminded his father of the letter about the scholarship from the *Star* between bites. His father listened in silence, shaking his head occasionally.

"Do you want to go to the academy?" Bigjim asked. "I thought you might like to work with me in the woods. I've let you stay in school much longer than almost any boy on the Creek, but Bob and Osk both said you were a right smart boy. I reckon maybe they were right, if that big newspaper thinks you are smart enough for them to pay for schooling."

Littlejim was not sure if his father was asking a question or making a statement. Perhaps, he thought, his father was not sure either. Littlejim could only answer, "Yes, Papa, more than anything in the world."

"Then I think you should open the letter, don't you?" his father asked as he picked up his coffee cup and walked out of the kitchen. "I'll sit with 'Trude for a while, I think."

Littlejim watched his father walk down the short hallway, his shoulders drooping as they had the day Mama became ill.

Finally opening his pocketknife, he used it as a letter opener and shook the folded paper to open it. Glancing at the words, he tried to find out what the letter said without Geneva and Nell guessing what his feelings were.

" 'Congratulations,' " he read. " 'You have won second place in the essay contest sponsored by the *Star*. The prize carries with it a bank draft for one hundred dollars, which you should find enclosed. Your fine essay will be published along with the first-place winner during the week of the presidential election in November. Congratulations again. Sincerely....'

"I didn't win the scholarship," he said, his throat tight with disappointment. Closing his eyes, he forced the tears forming there to stay in them. Crumpling the paper and throwing it into the wood box, where it could be used for kindling to start the morning fire, he got up from the table and walked to the door leading outside.

"I am so sorry," said Aunt Geneva, grasping his arm and hugging it. "Your essay was so fine. It deserved to win."

"I'm so sorry you didn't win," said Nell. "But you have a hundred dollars. I have never *seen* a hundred dollars. What will you buy with that?"

"A hundred dollars?!" Littlejim grabbed the rumpled envelope and smoothed it on the table. Reaching inside, he found a bank draft and read the amount written on it.

Smiling weakly at Nell, he said, "I guess I'd better tell Papa and Mama."

He paused outside the door to his parents' room and took a deep breath. Hearing strange voices, he hesitated, then pushed the door open just a crack so that he could see. The two doctors, Dr. Mr. Sloop and Dr. Mrs. Sloop, stood at the foot of Mama's bed. He had not heard them. They always came through the front door.

As the door creaked, Mama saw Littlejim and called to him. "James has told me you have a letter from the *Star.* I trust it is good news," she said.

"I won a hundred dollars. Papa can use the money I won for your medicine," he said.

"No," said Bigjim and Mama at the same time.

"The money is yours," said Mama. "For your education."

"We'll find a way to pay the doctors," said Papa. "You must use your money for school."

Dr. Mr. Sloop turned to Littlejim and said, "One of the reasons we dropped by so late this evening is to share the news that we will be moving to Crossnore soon, where we will build a boarding school for students who wish to continue their education beyond the local schools. We thought you might be interested in attending our new school."

Littlejim's heart lifted. "Would a hundred dollars pay for your school? It's not enough to pay for me to go to the academy for more than one year."

"That will cover the tuition for several years in the school we plan," said Dr. Mrs. Sloop. "We plan for our students to work and earn their education. The school will be ready by next fall. That's only one year away. What do you think about that?"

"Then I can work in the woods with you, Papa," said Littlejim, "and save the money I earn. We can still use my prize money for Mama."

"No," said Bigjim, rising with great dignity to place his hand on his son's shoulder. "You earned that money. It will be used for your education, my son the scholar."

Littlejim had thought that only girls fainted, but as he looked, openmouthed, at his father, he felt so swimmy-headed that he thought he might be the first man on the Creek to faint.

Chapter 33

COURT WAS HELD in the school in Plumtree since the new school year was not scheduled to begin until the following week. The circuit judge would arrive from the county seat in his new auty-mobile. Both the judge and Mr. Farber were staying at Mrs. Franklin's boardinghouse in the nearby village of Spear, where Mr. Farber had been preparing for his appearance in support of Bigjim.

A letter had arrived from Myron's father asking about the progress made by his brother. Littlejim had helped his father write a long letter explaining all that had occurred, including their very successful day of trout fishing.

Littlejim dared not ask if he would be allowed to attend the session of court, but at supper the day before the opening, Bigjim told his son that he should dress in his Sunday best and be ready to depart soon after sunup. His son stopped eating his fried trout because he was so surprised.

All day as he and his sister had stood on the river-bank fishing for trout to tempt their mother's appetite, he had wondered what it would be like to go to court with his father. Last winter he had been allowed to attend the local court when Aunt Zony heard several cases. He had found the procedures interesting, especially when his aunt banged the gavel and announced the fines or rents due in a large, important voice he had never heard her use anywhere else.

And now, he realized as he became aware of the trout and coleslaw on his plate, he would get to see a real trial with a real judge, a man in a long black robe like the one he had seen in the *Star*. He began to eat rapidly so that he could heat water in the kettle on Mama's cookstove for a bath before the twilight air grew too cool. Perhaps he could convince Aunt Geneva to trim his hair, too. He wanted to look his best when he walked into the courtroom with his father and Mr. Farber.

The following morning he followed them proudly down the aisle of the classroom behind his father to their seats near the front of the room. The desks had been arranged in two columns, leaving a wide aisle down the center. Benches had been brought from the church for those involved in the proceedings, who would sit in the front three rows.

Soon Mr. Guinn and two other men walked in and sat on the opposite side of the room from Bigjim and his son. Littlejim tried not to look at the man who had so wronged his father, but he noticed that his father glowered in Mr. Guinn's direction.

As the judge took his seat, Littlejim was disappointed to see that he was dressed in a suit, much like the other men in the room. He called court into session, the bailiff made announcements, and one person then another walked up to take the stand beside the judge.

"All of them had timber stolen from them by Mr. Guinn and his henchman, Mr. Thorn," explained Mr. Farber to Littlejim in a loud whisper. "Unfortunately, Mr. Thorn is out of our reach."

As the day passed, the events in court grew less and less interesting until Littlejim found himself nodding in the warm sunlight that streamed through the windows. He was happy to hear the judge announce that they would adjourn for noonday dinner.

"Ah, lunch," said Mr. Farber, rubbing his hands together in anticipation. "I've never eaten so well as I have eaten these past two weeks. I cannot fit into my clothing. Philadelphia has few restaurants which can match the fresh fruits and vegetables, to say nothing of the trout—ah, the trout. I shall hate to return to the office when this case is finished."

"We do eat well," agreed Bigjim as they walked across the bridge to the Tea Room, which served, so the sign in the window said, "luncheon dishes."

"Geneva packed us a basket of dinner," said Bigjim as they passed his wagon.

"Today this is my treat to repay your kindness in

trout fishing with me and for the fine meals I've enjoyed this week at your home. I hope, of course, that you will invite me down here again, when we have no legal work to do."

"You will always be welcome," said Bigjim, offering his hand.

"And by the way, I think we have a chance of winning this. I think we have a solid case," said Mr. Farber.

After they were seated in the tea room, Littlejim watched his father, who seemed overwhelmed that they were going to eat in a public place. His legs were too long to fit under the table, and he did not seem to know what to do with the array of cutlery arranged at their plates. Littlejim did not know either, so he did not take his eyes off Mr. Farber. Ordering what Mr. Farber ordered and watching to see which fork Mr. Farber lifted, Littlejim was fairly sure he would not embarrass their host.

But Bigjim stared at the plate of food in front of him. Looking at his father frantically, Littlejim nodded as he lifted his fork. Finally Bigjim looked at his son, nodded, and lifted the same fork to eat slowly and awkwardly.

Littlejim suddenly realized that his father had probably never eaten in such a place before. He had always thought his father was the most powerful man on earth, that he knew best about everything; if his papa said it, it was so. But watching his father eat, the boy realized that his father was just a logger from the Creek community, who had rarely been out in the modern world.

No wonder he did not like all the changes. The changes in his world must frighten him. In his world on the Creek he was a leader, a respected man of the community, the best logger anyone knew. Here he was a man, ignorant about which fork to use, unlearned in the ways of the modern world.

Then Littlejim realized what great courage taking Mr. Guinn to court required on his father's part: courage not only to write and ask for help, but courage to face all the things he did not know and to go into a world where others might laugh at him for what he did not know. Littlejim remembered the family of sangers on the railroad platform that day with Myron. They were ridiculed for all they did not know. His father had shown courage enough to face the possibility of that same ridicule.

Littlejim was fairly bursting with pride, and with chocolate cake, when he heard Mr. Farber saying, "We were lucky to find that little-known law about property rights here in North Carolina. Not many states still have such laws on the books. I think we can get at least part of your money back."

"But you can't bring back my trees," said Bigjim sadly, as they made their way back to the makeshift courtroom. "It takes many lifetimes to bring back trees like those."

"True enough," said Mr. Farber. "But if we can stop this man, we may make others think twice about this kind of action. Your courage in standing up to them will make a difference. You saw how many men from all the surrounding counties were willing to come and testify about Guinn's tactics."

The afternoon passed slowly until at last Bigjim was called to take the stand. Littlejim listened to every word his father said. Speaking slowly and with great care in choosing his words, he told of Mama's illness and the need for money, of Myron's fears about the contract, and the devastation of having his best stand of timber cut without his knowledge or permission.

"That stand of timber was being saved for the most important thing in my life," said Bigjim, looking across the room at his son. "Those trees were being saved to pay for my son's education, so he can go on to the academy or even to college, if he's a mind to. He's the finest scholar on the Creek, and I aimed to give him the privileges I never had."

Littlejim could hardly believe the words he was hearing. His heart swelled as he listened to his father's voice saying, "And if he does not want to go to school, the trees would be passed on to him, and to his sons, and to their sons. There be no trees of that size left anywhere now. And for my son's children it may be that these hills will be barren like those Ian tells of in Scotland, thanks to thieves who have no respect for their neighbors nor for the land."

When Bigjim had finished, he walked slowly and with great dignity back to sit beside Littlejim. Littlejim reached out to shake his father's hand, trying to make the tears of joy remain in his eyes instead of allowing them to fall on their hands and embarrass his father.

"Son," was the only word Bigjim spoke as he sat down.

When the hearing was over, the judge announced, "And Dearborne Guinn, you will pay James Houston the sum of one thousand dollars in damages, and you will return all mineral rights to him. You will pay the other plaintiffs in kind. You will do this within thirty days from this day's date or you will spend an amount of time in jail, the length of which will be determined by your eagerness to pay this amount to the victims of your schemes. Case closed."

Mr. Farber was smiling as the judge stepped down from his place behind the teacher's desk to shake hands with him.

"I'll challenge you to another game of rummy anytime you are in this neck of the woods," the judge said with a wink.

"Then you'll join us on our next trout-fishing expedition to these mountains?" asked Mr. Farber.

The judge nodded as he moved to shake hands with Littlejim, who had to listen carefully when the man spoke softly to him. Later he was sure he had heard the words correctly: "You are one lucky young man, my boy. Every boy should have a father who loves his son as much as your father loves you. Yes, you are one lucky young man."

Littlejim drew himself up to his full height and walked with great dignity, his head held high, beside his papa as they made their way down the aisle through the crowded room toward the door.

It just might be, he thought, that the judge was right.

Chapter 34

As Littlejim carefully carried a heavy crock of Aunt Geneva's lemonade down the kitchen steps, he looked around the front yard of his home. He had never seen so many people gathered there. People had come from churches in Plumtree, Powder Mill, and some from as far away as Bakersville and Pine Grove to be a part of the all-day singing and dinner-on-the-ground.

Usually such gatherings were held at one of the churches and attended by the congregations from other churches in the area. At the homecoming for a family or congregation, such gatherings might be held at a family cemetery. But on the last bright Sunday in September, with a tang of fall's chill in the air, Preacher Hall had asked his flock to gather at the Houston farm to celebrate Gertrude's return from the hospital, as well as Bigjim's triumph over the mineral speculators in court. Littlejim was grateful to the minister, who knew that Mama was still too weak to ride the wagon to church.

Mr. Farber, enticed by the prospect of more trout fishing the following Monday, had been persuaded to stay for the celebration. He had taken off his jacket and tie, rolled up his sleeves, and helped Bigjim, Tarp, and Bob carry every table and chair in the house out into the yard as Littlejim and Nell carried the sawhorses from the woodshed and placed new boards across them to form even more tables.

All dressed up in a clean, starched shirt and necktie, and wearing his good suit coat over his brand-new overalls, Bigjim's family had never seen him in such an expansive mood. He had sent Littlejim and the wagon to Plumtree yesterday to buy one of the last blocks of ice in Mr. Burleson's icehouse to make ice cream to be served after the singing. Now Littlejim was sure that the block of ice would not supply all the ice-cream churns, new machines introduced to the area by Burleson's Store, their guests had brought. That did not seem to bother his father. He could see that his father was *almost* smiling as he welcomed each vehicle as it drove up the hill and into the barnyard. Shaking hands with each man who arrived, he accepted their congratulations and led many of the women through the meadow gate to the side yard, where Mama sat smiling happily, a quilt across her knees to guard against a chill, under the big red-cherry tree.

As the horses, wagons, buggies, and three—Littlejim could hardly believe his eyes as they came chugging up the Creek Road—*three* automobiles were arriving at the gathering, Mr. Farber walked up to stand beside him. Littlejim's head was swimming with the excitement of three automobiles and with watching for one blond girl to arrive.

"Three *auty-mobiles!*" Littlejim said in wonder, pronouncing the word carefully. "At our house."

Mr. Farber interrupted his thoughts. "Automobiles all over the place. Henson Creek will soon qualify as a city." Then, seeing the boy's troubled expression, he added, "I speak in jest. But changing the subject, I've never seen so much food."

Littlejim smiled and nodded his head. Every woman in the valley must have been cooking for days, he thought. The tables had been filled an hour ago, and tablecloths had been spread under the apple trees in the side yard and in the meadow near the road. Two campfires had been built in the pasture field up the hill from the barn to make coffee and heat the black kettles filled with chicken and dumplings, fresh vegetables, and stewed apples. The fragrances melded and gave the air a fine perfume that made Littlejim's mouth water.

"Do we eat soon?" asked Mr. Farber. "The fragrances of food may overwhelm me."

"As soon as the preacher says grace," answered Littlejim, only half hearing the question. He had spotted the blond-haired girl for whom he had been watching all morning, Mr. Tom Greene's daughter. The

Greenes had come after all. He could see them placing their baskets and kettles near Mama's herb beds beside the kitchen door. Watching the family walk over to greet Mama, he waved shyly and felt his heart leap as he caught a shy return wave while two green eyes smiled back at him. "Then the singing begins. It goes on all afternoon until sundown," he added quickly, hoping that he had not been rude to their guest.

"Who's Grace?" asked Mr. Farber. "Will Grace sing?"

Littlejim was startled by the question. He turned to Mr. Farber, puzzled. "Grace?" he said. "I don't know anyone here named *Grace*," he said. "Grace?"

"You said that as soon as the preacher says, 'Grace,' we can eat," said Mr. Farber, who seemed to be as puzzled as Littlejim. "Who is Grace? And why does the preacher have to say her name so we can eat? Who *is* Grace? She must be very important!"

Littlejim began to laugh. "I'm sorry," he said. "Saying grace means saying thank you to God for the food. I guess it means that we ask for blessings on the food and on us, too. You don't use the word in Philadelphia, I guess?"

Mr. Farber was laughing, too. "No," he said. "We don't say 'grace' before we eat, but I think it's a nice custom. I can hardly wait to tell my friend, Grace Langstrom, about it. Myron explained that the language differences here often pose problems with outsiders. Now I think I know what he means."

The preacher was walking over to stand beside
Mama and was calling for everyone to gather around
him. Littlejim motioned for Mr. Farber to follow him to
the side yard, and they stood beside Bigjim, who was
standing tall beside Mama's chair and holding May, who
sat on his arm. Nell stood with Aunt Geneva, Tarp, Bob,
and Galen while the rest of the family stood nearby.
Out of the corner of his eye Littlejim could see that the
Tom Greenes, who had been visiting with Mama when
the preacher called, were standing with his family. He
looked at the ground to hide a smile. Perhaps when the
singing began, he would ask Ruth to walk with him down
to the springhouse to bring up ice for the ice cream.

"Before we say grace," Preacher Hall said genially,
"our host would like to say a few words." He made a
slight bow to Bigjim, who handed May to Uncle Bob.
"Mr. Houston, thank you for your invitation to celebrate
with you this fine Sunday morning."

Bigjim cleared his throat and looked around him.
Littlejim was standing so close that he could see that his
father's hands were shaking as he clasped them in front
of him.

"My friends and neighbors," Bigjim began. "This is
a thankful day for me and for my family. We are glad-
dened that you could help us to say our thanks for all
the blessings bestowed on us this day." He took Mama's
hand in his as she smiled up at him, looking as if a
candle had been lit so that it glowed inside her face.
"My good wife, Gertrude, here, is back with us." His

voice quivered and his son could see tears glistening in his eyes. "She grows stronger each day. We are a family again." Bigjim paused. "Amen."

Several voices echoed around the yard, the meadow, and the pasture: "Amen."

"And Mr. Farber here"—dropping Mama's hand, Bigjim walked over to shake the attorney's hand—"Mr. Farber has come to our aid, to help us to fight iniquity, to stand on the side of the righteous again' the mineral speculators and outlaws who would take our land and our timber."

Littlejim smiled secretly. He could almost read Mama's thoughts: "Yah, Jim, you are getting wound up. Are you going to preach us a fine sermon?" Littlejim had heard Mama speak those words when his papa felt intensely about something. Now he began to wonder, too. He had never heard his father talk so much in one day in his whole life.

He smiled at Aunt Geneva, thinking that she might say his father was as pickled as the chickens who drank the fermented cherries by the joy of celebrating Mama's return home. Becoming a bit uncomfortable with his father's unaccustomed long-winded discourse, he was wishing that his father would finish his speech so that they could eat, when the sound of his own name interrupted his thoughts.

"And my fine son, Jimmy," his father was saying. "You all know he is a fine writer, the winner of competitions, with his words printed in a big-city news-paper." Bigjim took a well-worn newspaper page from the bib pocket of his overalls and pointed to Littlejim's essay. Littlejim could hardly believe what he was seeing—or hearing. "My son wrote one of his fine pieces in a letter to young Mr. Farber from Philadelphia. He wrote such a fine letter that it was printed in the *Philadelphia Inquirer,* and his uncle was sent to help us to seek justice in a court of law. And although hard cash can never"—Bigjim paused—"*never* bring back that stand of virgin timber, we received justice under the law."

Littlejim was not sure he had heard his father's words correctly. He leaned forward to listen more carefully. His father had just called him his fine son! He blinked his eyes and shook his head to make sure he was not dreaming.

"And don't you deny it, Jimmy," his father was saying, assuming that the boy was disavowing his part in bringing help from Philadelphia. Startled, Littlejim's face grew fiery with embarrassment and elation at his father's attention.

"Young Houston wrote such a fine letter defending his father's position that any man of integrity would have been compelled to come to his aid," added Mr. Farber. "My partner's son, the Houstons' summer guest, supported the case with his observations, and the readers of the *Inquirer* were moved to send financial aid. The remainder of the money will be used for Mrs. Houston's medical treatment, and so here we are celebrating our victory!"

"A victory that would have been impossible without the work of my son," added Bigjim, lifting his son's hand in his. "And, son"—he stopped, turning to look at Littlejim and searching for words as he brought their hands down in front of Mama—"you are right much of a man. This day I honor you. One of the things I have to be thankful for this day is a fine son with a fine mind who uses that mind for good."

Littlejim stood, his eyes wide and his lips parted in surprise.

The greatest dream of all had come true for Littlejim. His papa had said, here in front of every person assembled, that he was right much of a man. Straightening his shoulders to stand as tall as his papa, Littlejim glanced around at Mama, tears of happiness on her cheeks, to see her reach for both their hands. The two men dropped their hands to join theirs with hers.

Then, reaching out to take his son's hand again, Bigjim nodded. Everyone in the circle joined hands, the joining making a wave that traveled through the meadow, the barnyard, and the orchard, reaching Littlejim's free hand. Nell placed her small hand in her brother's big one as the girl with the green eyes smiled proudly across the yard at him.

Littlejim was startled as his father turned to him and added as the circle, snaking around the entire farm, was finished, "And I promise with everything that is in me, I will work to help you see that you make your dreams come true, whether that dream is to be a scholar, to be an aviator, or to be the first man to walk on the moon. I will see that you get the education I never got, my son."

Bigjim bowed his head quickly to hide his face as Preacher Hall said, "Amen."

As Preacher Hall led the prayer, Littlejim's thoughts were racing to all his possible futures, but his lips whispered silently, "Thank you, Papa. You have made the most important dream of all come true."

When Preacher Hall had finished, Littlejim said aloud only, "Thank you, Papa."

Further Reading

Caruso, J. A. *The Appalachian Frontier.* New York: Bobbs-Merrill, 1959.

Kephart, H. *Our Southern Highlanders: A Narrative of Adventure in the Southern Appalachians and a Study of Life among the Mountaineers.* Knoxville: The University of Tennessee Press, 1913, 1990.

McWhiney, G. *Cracker Culture: Celtic Ways in the Old South.* Tuscaloosa: University of Alabama Press, 1988.

Raitz, K. B., R. Ulack, and T. R. Leinbach. *Appalachia: A Regional Geography, Land, People and Development.* Boulder, Colo.: Westview Press, 1984.

Williams, C. D. *Southern Mountain Speech.* Berea, Ky.: Berea College Press, 1992.

——. *The Southern Mountaineer in Fact and Fiction.* Dissertation. New York: New York University, 1961.

Williamson, J. W. *Hillbillyland: What the Movies Did to the Mountains and What the Mountains Did to the Movies.* Chapel Hill: University of North Carolina Press, 1995.

Wolfram, W., and D. Christian. *Appalachian Speech.* Arlington, Va.: Center for Applied Linguistics, 1976.

Wolfram, W., D. Christian, and N. Dube. *Variation and Change in Geographically Isolated Communities: Appalachian English and Ozark English.* Tuscaloosa: University of Alabama Press/American Dialect Society, 1987.

HOUGHTON COLLEGE LIBRARY - Houghton, NY

1000249039